JESS THE BORDER COLLIE
The Betrayal

'... one's talking about it,' Fiona said. 'We all know ... the fire started – that *you* burned down your ... s Windy Hill.' Fiona's eyes narrowed. 'So how ... feel about that, Jenny Miles?' she challenged.

'... it's not true!' Jenny protested.

'... ie took a step forward to defend Jenny, but J... ahead of her. Placing himself between Jenny a... ona, he stood there stiffly, growling up at the ... irl.

Fi... a stepped back quickly as Jess gave a sharp bark ... oved towards her. 'Call that dog off!' she cried i... a rising voice. 'He's going to bite me!'

'Jess wouldn't bite anybody,' Jenny said.

Fiona looked at her, her face flushed. 'Yeah, and you ... n't start fires, do you?' she said, then she turned on h... heel and marched off back to her father.

'... tood there, still growling softly, and Jenny bent to ... assure him.

'Don't take any notice of her, Jenny,' Carrie said, fro... ning.

'... looked up at her. 'Do you think what she sai... true? Does everyone think it was my fault?'

JESS
THE BORDER COLLIE

THE BETRAYAL

LUCY DANIELS

ILLUSTRATED BY SHEILA RATCLIFFE

**Hodder
Children's
Books**

a division of Hodder Headline plc

Special thanks to Helen Magee

Text copyright © 1999 Ben M. Baglio
Created by Ben M. Baglio, London W12 7QY
Illustrations copyright © 1999 Sheila Ratcliffe

First published in Great Britain in 1999
by Hodder Children's Books

A Catalogue record for this book is available from the British Library

ISBN 0 340 73595 3

Typeset by Avon Dataset Ltd, Bidford-on-Avon, Warks

Printed and bound in Great Britain by
The Guernsey Press Co. Ltd, Channel Isles

Hodder Children's Books
a division of Hodder Headline plc
338 Euston Road
London NW1 3BH

1

'We're going to have a great party tonight, Jess!' Jenny Miles said, as she gazed up at the towering bonfire, which was waiting to be lit.

Jess, her black and white Border collie, looked up at her, his head to one side, and Jenny laughed. 'OK, I know what you're waiting for,' she said, picking up a stick. 'Go find, boy!'

Jenny tossed the stick high in the air for him. The young sheepdog scampered off across the field as Jenny watched the stick arc high in the blue November sky. From up here, above Windy Hill, her family's farm in the Scottish borders, Jenny could see Puffin Island, lying like a green jewel off the coast, its cliffs sparkling in the morning sun. The wind from the sea blew her shoulder-length fair hair across her eyes and caught at the stick she had thrown. It sailed over the drystone wall that separated Windy Hill's land from Dunraven, the neighbouring farm.

Jenny spotted a tall dark-haired girl and a little boy walking down the track on the other side of the wall. It was Fiona McLay and her brother, Paul. Toby, his brown and black Border terrier, was at his side. 'Oh no!' Jenny gasped. 'Watch out!'

The stick fell, just grazing Fiona's arm. She immediately turned towards Jenny, her mouth set in an angry line. 'You did that deliberately, Jenny Miles,' she accused, as Jenny ran over towards them. Fiona McLay's father owned Dunraven. He and Fraser Miles, Jenny's father, had never been friends and Fiona tried to pick fights with Jenny whenever she could.

'I didn't, Fiona,' Jenny protested. 'I'm sorry. Are you hurt?'

'As if you care!' Fiona replied.

'It was an accident, Fiona,' Paul put in. 'Jenny didn't mean to hit you.'

Fiona glanced down at her eight-year-old brother. 'Don't interfere, Paul,' she snapped. Then she turned on her heel and walked off down the track. 'Come on, Paul!'

Paul looked after her, his wide grey eyes unhappy. 'I want to talk to Jenny about the bonfire party,' he called.

Fiona whirled round. 'Oh, yes – the famous Windy Hill bonfire party,' she scoffed, nastily. 'Don't expect *me* to come. I know you only invited me because you *had* to!'

'I don't want you to come anyway!' Jenny called after her. She was so angry at Fiona's rudeness that she spoke without thinking.

'Are you all right?' Paul asked, scrambling over the wall, Toby following at his heels. 'Did Fiona upset you?'

Jenny smiled at the little boy. 'It's all right, Paul, it's not your fault,' she said, stroking Jess's head. She picked up the stick and threw it for the collie.

Jess and Toby immediately scampered after it.

'Doesn't Jess run fast?' said Paul. 'He's faster than Toby now, even *with* his bad leg!'

Jenny nodded and smiled. Jess had been born with a badly twisted leg. Fraser Miles had thought that putting the puppy down would be kindest, since he would never make a working dog, but Jenny had pleaded for Jess's life and nursed him through an operation to straighten his leg.

Jenny's dedication and Jess's courage had paid off. Now Jess was as lively as any other dog, and he had proved a great help with the lambing last spring. Even Jenny's father admitted that Jess had been worth saving.

Paul's eyes shifted across the field to the wood pile that was to be the bonfire. 'Wow!' he said. 'It's enormous! Have you got a guy as well?'

Jenny nodded. 'We've just got to finish making him,' she said. 'We'll put him on the top of the bonfire just before we light it.'

'I know all about Guy Fawkes Night and why we have bonfires and fireworks and guys,' Paul said proudly. 'We learned a rhyme about it at school: "Remember, remember, the fifth of

November, gunpowder, treason and plot!" '

Jenny laughed. 'Did you learn what the plot was?' she asked.

Paul nodded. 'Hundreds of years ago some men who didn't like the government tried to blow up the Houses of Parliament with a barrel of gunpowder. And they were led by a man called Guy Fawkes.'

Jenny nodded, smiling. She looked at the two dogs, chasing each other round the bonfire. 'You mustn't bring Toby tonight, Paul,' she warned him.

Paul shook his head. 'The fireworks would scare him. I'll leave him at home. Who else is coming to the party?'

'Matt's coming home,' Jenny told him. 'He's bringing his new girlfriend with him. She's on the same course as him.' Matt was Jenny's nineteen-year-old brother. He was away at agricultural college, but he came home as often as he could to help on the farm. 'And lots of my new friends from school are coming too,' Jenny went on. She had recently started senior school in Greybridge, the local market town. 'You'll like them.'

'Fiona doesn't like them,' Paul announced. 'She says she hates the new school.'

Fiona was in the same class as Jenny at Greybridge School, but they had little to do with each other.

'She's got a project to do,' Paul went on. 'It's all about drawing a map of where you live with routes marked to all your friends' houses. She says she can't be bothered with it.'

Jenny was surprised. 'That's our Geography project,' she explained. 'Most people are really enjoying it. It's fun.'

'Fiona doesn't think so,' Paul said. He looked round and whistled for Toby. 'I'd better go. Fiona will be angry if she has to wait for me.'

Jenny sighed as she watched Paul and Toby run off. Fiona *was* difficult. She had scared Paul so badly when he had needed to go into hospital for an ear operation that the little boy had run away. Jess had found Paul at Darktarn Keep further up the hill and had then helped rescue the little boy when he had fallen into the river below. At first Fiona had been so relieved that Paul was all right that she'd made a special effort to be nice to him. But it hadn't lasted long and now it seemed she was back to her old self, bossing Paul around.

Jenny sighed and whistled for Jess. The collie came racing across the short grass towards her. 'Come on, boy,' she cried. 'We've got work to do! And Matt is coming home!'

A motorbike was drawing up in the farmyard as Jenny and Jess hurtled down the track. Matt! But two leather-clad figures sat astride the bike. Who was with him? Matt parked the bike and took off his helmet. He put out a hand to help his companion off the back of the bike, before turning to unload a couple of bags out of the side-paniers. Jenny raced across the farmyard and threw herself at her brother.

'Hi, Jen,' Matt laughed, dropping the bags on the cobbles of the yard and giving his sister a bear hug. He stood away from her and ruffled her hair – his way of affectionately teasing his younger sister. Behind him, a slim girl was taking off her helmet and smoothing down her fair hair. Matt looked back at her and smiled. 'How about saying hello to Vicky, Jen?'

Jenny turned to the girl and held out her hand. 'Hi, Vicky,' she said. 'Welcome to Windy Hill!'

Vicky took Jenny's hand and shook it firmly, then she looked down at Jess. Tail wagging, the Border collie leaped up at her.

'Down, Jess!' Jenny commanded.

Vicky laughed. 'Oh, I don't mind,' she said, her bright hazel eyes twinkling. 'I've heard all about the famous Jess from Matt. He really is a gorgeous dog.'

Jenny beamed at Vicky. Nothing pleased her more than people complimenting Jess – and Jess obviously liked Vicky.

The farmhouse door opened and Fraser Miles strode across the cobbled yard towards them. He held out his hand to Vicky in greeting and then hugged his son. With his dark colouring and startling blue eyes, he and Matt were very alike. Two black and white sheepdogs trotted at Fraser's heels.

'That's Jake and Nell,' Matt told Vicky. 'They're the best working dogs in the Borders – but their greatest claim to fame as far as Jenny's concerned is that they're Jess's parents!'

Vicky laughed as Jess barked then raced up to the two older dogs and began to run around them, wagging his tail. Jake and Nell butted him playfully but they didn't chase him. They were working dogs and they behaved like working dogs. Jess scampered off towards the kitchen door just as Mrs Grace, the housekeeper, came out into the yard.

'What do you think of the lambing barn now that it's finished and painted, Matt?' she asked, after the introductions had been made.

Matt swung round to look at the new barn his father had built with the profits from the last lambing. Its fresh green paint sparkled in the sun. 'It looks great,' he said approvingly. 'Last time I was here it still needed its roof putting on. It looks a lot better than the old one.' Matt turned to Vicky. 'The old lambing barn had been falling to bits for years,' he explained. 'It finally blew down in a gale, last winter. This one is much better.'

Fraser Miles looked pleased. 'It's going to be really useful to us this winter,' he said. 'I've got some of the young pregnant ewes in there already. And it will make the lambing so much easier.'

Fraser Miles had a thousand Scottish Blackface sheep on his farm. He had put the rams into the fields with the ewes in October and now most of the flock were pregnant. Scottish Blackfaces were a hardy hill breed and their thick coats were perfectly suited to the harsh Border winters but, even so, pregnant ewes, especially those expecting lambs for the first time, needed a lot of looking after.

'I bet this spring's lambing is going to be even better than last year's,' Jenny said, looking at her father.

'If it's as good as the last lambing, I'll be happy,' Fraser responded. 'Things are certainly looking good so far.'

Jenny smiled, delighted to see her father so optimistic. Sheep farming was Fraser Miles's whole life. It was a hard life but he loved it.

'Come and have something to eat,' Mrs Grace urged them. 'I've been baking for two days for this bonfire party, so there's plenty.'

'You don't have to ask twice,' Matt joked, heading for the kitchen door.

'Carrie arrived not long ago, too,' Mrs Grace said to Jenny. 'She's gone over to the shearing shed to help Ian with making the guy. They're bound to be hungry.'

Jenny grinned. 'Ian's always hungry,' she said, as she and Jess made for the shearing shed. Ian Amery was Ellen Grace's nephew. He had come to stay with his aunt when his parents had gone to Canada. Ellen and Ian had come to live at Windy Hill when Calum McLay had turned Ellen out of the cottage she had rented on Dunraven land.

'Hi, Jen,' Carrie said. 'Look at this. It's going to be the best guy in the world!' she announced as she stuffed straw into the sack that made up the guy's body.

Jenny smiled. Carrie had come to live in Cliffbay, a nearby fishing village, the previous year. She was now Jenny's best friend.

'Can you hold the bottoms of the trouser legs, while I tie some string round them, Jen?' Ian said. 'We don't want the straw falling out.'

Jenny held the bottoms of the old pair of trousers as Ian tightened the string and knotted it. 'Mrs Grace says we've to come in for something to eat,' she said.

Ian looked up. 'Great!' he said. 'I'm starving. We can finish the guy later. We've got loads of

time before tonight – and have you *seen* the piles of food Aunt Ellen has made?'

The big farmhouse kitchen was bright with winter sunlight. Red checked curtains hung at the window and the blue and white crockery on the dresser gleamed. The flagged floor was bright with warm rag rugs and Jess's basket was tucked away in one corner, his favourite blue woollen blanket folded inside. Smells of baking filled the air and the Aga gave off a comforting heat after the chill of the sea wind.

'I'm really going to miss your cooking when I go to Canada for Christmas, Aunt Ellen,' Ian said, as he sat down at the big kitchen table. 'But at least I'm going to learn to ski – that'll be great.'

'Skiing,' Jenny sighed. 'I've never been skiing.'

Ian grinned at her. 'I'll teach you when I come back from Canada,' he promised. 'We can go up by Darktarn Keep if there's enough snow this winter.'

'Tell me about a winter when there hasn't been plenty of snow in these parts,' Mrs Grace joked.

'We had a bad winter on our farm too,' Vicky said.

Fraser looked at her in surprise. 'Matt didn't tell us you came from a farming family,' he said.

'I told her to keep quiet about it,' Matt laughed. 'I warned her she'd get dragged in to help if she admitted to being a farmer's daughter.'

Jenny gave him a dig in the ribs as he sat down at the table beside her. Vicky told Fraser and the others about the farm her parents owned.

'A sheep farm – like this?' Ian exclaimed.

'But on the other side of the border,' Vicky said with mock seriousness. 'The English side.'

'Uh-oh,' said Carrie. 'That means you and the Mileses are probably old enemies. Your ancestors probably stole each other's sheep.'

Vicky laughed. 'I suppose we did,' she said.

Jenny looked round the table. Everyone was talking and laughing and having a great time – and tonight at the bonfire there would be even more people.

'By the way, Mum is bringing loads of toffee apples for the party,' Carrie said.

'That'll be a help,' Mrs Grace approved. 'With

all the school friends you two have invited, we'll need them.'

Jenny smiled. 'Amy Jarrow says she hasn't had an invitation to any other bonfire parties so she'll come.'

'Charming!' said Ian.

Carrie spluttered with laughter. 'Amy is always putting her foot in it,' she said. 'She doesn't mean to sound rude. She's nice, really.'

'Her dad is going to drive a crowd of them over from Greybridge,' Jenny said.

A warm, wet tongue licked her hand and Jenny looked down. Jess was gazing up at her with soulful eyes. 'All right,' she whispered. 'Just this once.' She fed him a chunk of scone from her plate.

Jess gulped it down, then he laid his head on Jenny's lap. 'Oh, Jess,' Jenny said. 'It's such a pity you'll have to miss the bonfire tonight, but the fireworks would frighten you. I'll save you some sausages, though – I promise.'

Fraser Miles looked up and smiled at her. 'Do you remember how much your mum loved bonfire night?' he asked softly.

Jenny nodded. 'Everyone is really glad we've

decided to hold our traditional bonfire party again. They missed having it last year. Mum made it famous . . .' Jenny felt a sudden wave of sadness, remembering why there hadn't been a Windy Hill bonfire party the previous year. Her mother, Sheena Miles, had been killed in a riding accident a few months before.

Tonight's celebration, the first without Sheena, wouldn't be quite the same. But Jenny had asked her father specially if they could have a bonfire party. She was sure her mother would have liked that.

'I reckon we'll have to keep its reputation up then,' Matt put in, squeezing Jenny's arm.

Jenny smiled and nodded. 'We'll make it the best bonfire night ever!'

2

Jenny dashed up to her bedroom early that evening to fetch her old padded jacket. Her father had given her a new jacket for her birthday two weeks earlier but she didn't want to get it all smoky from the bonfire.

She cast a glance round her bedroom. Its yellow painted walls were covered with posters but, in pride of place above her bed, was the sketch Carrie's mother had drawn of Jess when he was just a few months old. He looked so appealing, with his front leg still in the plaster cast he'd worn after his operation.

Jenny picked up her woolly hat and scarf and opened the wardrobe door to look for her jacket. Just then, her bedroom light went out.

'It's all right, it's probably just a fuse blown,' Matt called from downstairs. 'I'll have it fixed in a moment.'

Jenny rummaged in the wardrobe but it was so dark, she couldn't see a thing. Then she had an idea. 'My candles!' she exclaimed, feeling her way across to her desk by the window. The desk was piled with papers for her Geography project. Jenny reached across them to the windowsill and felt around for the fat pink candle and box of matches she knew was there. Striking a match, she lit the candle and smiled ruefully. Matt had given her the candle-making kit for her birthday. Her initial attempts at candle making hadn't been too successful, to say the least! The first one had collapsed all over the kitchen table. This one was a *little* better. Jenny cleared a space and set it in the middle of the desk. She had just found her jacket when the light went on again and she heard feet on the stairs. Her father popped his head round her bedroom door.

'Come on, lass,' he said. 'People are beginning to arrive! Don't forget to put that candle out.'

Jenny hastily blew out the candle and made for the door. She couldn't wait for the bonfire party to start!

Jess was already out in the yard, tail wagging, greeting the guests. Jenny smiled as she saw the fuss everyone made of him.

Tom Palmer, the vet who had looked after Jess when he was a puppy, rubbed the collie's ears. 'How's my favourite sheepdog?' he said as Jess leaped up at him.

The Turners' car drew into the yard and Jess was off again, leaping up at Pam and Gordon Turner, Carrie's parents, as they unloaded boxes of toffee apples from the boot.

Amy Jarrow's father was the last to arrive, and a crowd of youngsters spilled out of the back of his minibus.

'I don't think I'll ever get Jess inside,' Jenny laughed, as Amy and the others began to play with him.

'You'll have to, lass,' her father said. 'We can't

have him outside with fireworks around.'

Jenny nodded and called to Jess. The Border collie came running towards her, barking excitedly. 'Come on, boy,' Jenny said. 'Time to see you safely inside.'

Fraser was organising everyone into teams to shift the provisions from the kitchen to the jeep. 'Ready, Jenny?' he called as he loaded the portable barbecue.

Jenny shook her head. 'I just want to make sure Jess is all right,' she said. 'He's quite excited with all these people around. I'll wait and see that he's settled. You go on ahead. I'll catch up.'

Mr Miles nodded.

'I've checked on Jake and Nell,' Matt said, walking up to the jeep with Vicky. 'They're safely shut in the stable with Mercury.'

'And the breeding ewes?' Mr Miles asked.

Matt nodded. 'They're all in the pens in the lambing barn.' He turned to Jenny. 'Don't be too long, Jen,' he called as he and Vicky climbed into the jeep. 'You don't want to miss any of the fun!'

'I won't,' Jenny called back. She waved as Matt and Vicky drove off in the jeep, following the road round to the top field where the bonfire stood, waiting to be lit.

Fraser, Mrs Grace, Carrie, Ian and the others cut across the fields on foot. It was dark but her father led the way and they all had torches.

Jenny led Jess into the kitchen and settled him down in his basket. He was still excitable and it took quite a while to calm him down. 'I know you want to come with me, Jess,' she said. 'But, really, this is for your own good. I'll come down and see you in a little while.'

Jess whined and put a paw on Jenny's knee, looking up at her pleadingly. 'I'll be back,' she promised, backing out of the door. Feeling a little guilty, she closed the door carefully behind her.

Turning towards the track, Jenny switched on her torch. The bright beam lit up the way ahead. Jenny snuggled into her jacket, pulling her scarf up round her ears. The wind had dropped but the air smelt frosty and crisp. Perfect weather for a bonfire, she said to herself as she set off for the top field.

'I've got the barbecue going,' Matt announced

as Jenny arrived. 'It's just about ready for cooking.'

'Time for me to get started,' Mrs Grace said. 'Hand me that plastic container, Jenny, and I'll get the sausages on.'

Carrie and Ian had unloaded the boxes of food on to a table next to the barbecue.

'Wow!' said Ian, looking at the array of sandwiches and rolls. 'There's enough here to feed an army.'

'You'll be all right then, Ian,' Pam Turner joked, as she dumped a box of toffee apples on the table.

Ian grinned. 'I've just got a healthy appetite, that's all,' he said.

'Time to light the bonfire, Jenny,' Fraser Miles shouted over.

Carrie was dancing with impatience. 'Come on, Jen!' she called. 'Everyone's waiting!'

Jenny hurried over to join the dozens of people huddled round to watch the lighting of the bonfire. Matt and Vicky had put the guy on top of the pile of old fence posts and wood and it looked magnificently eerie. Fraser took a box of matches and lit a long taper. He held it out to

Jenny. 'Would you like to do it?' he asked, smiling.

Jenny nodded and took the taper. She felt a lump in her throat as she thought of her mother and how much she would have enjoyed this.

Mr Miles pointed to a heap of white blocks nestled in paper and tucked into the bonfire. 'Put the taper just there,' he advised. 'Those are firelighters so they should get the fire started pretty easily.'

Jenny's hand shook a little as she touched the taper to the firelighters. At once a blue flame sprang up and swept throughout the bed of paper and twigs. It reached the smaller branches and began to crackle as the flames caught and ran like red and yellow tongues through the middle of the bonfire. There was a cheer, followed by clapping from the assembled crowd as the fire took hold and the bonfire leapt into life.

'Well done, Jenny,' Gordon and Pam Turner called out to her.

Jenny smiled and shoved her hands in her pockets. She cast a look around all their guests as they stood happily watching the bonfire flames reach up into the sky.

'How's Jess?' Matt asked as he and Vicky came to stand beside Jenny. Matt had his arm round Vicky's shoulder and she snuggled close to him, smiling up at him. It was good to see Matt looking so relaxed and happy.

'He wasn't too pleased to be left at home,' Jenny replied. 'But I'll go down and see him in a while – just to make sure he doesn't feel left out. Poor thing, he couldn't understand why I had to lock him in the kitchen.'

'He must wonder what's going on,' Vicky said sympathetically.

'He'll forgive you – if you take him some sausages,' Matt said with a twinkle in his eye.

'Make that *lots* of sausages,' Carrie put in.

'I'm going to take some for Nell and Jake too,' said Jenny.

'Will you have a look at Mercury while you're there?' Matt asked.

'Sure thing,' Jenny said, 'and I'll take him an apple.'

'How about giving Mrs Grace a hand with the barbecue, first?' Carrie suggested. 'She looks pretty busy.'

'Good idea,' agreed Jenny. She sniffed as they walked towards the barbecue. 'It smells great already.'

'We've come to help,' Carrie said as they approached Mrs Grace.

Ellen Grace smiled at them and scooped a load of sausages off the barbecue and on to a large platter. 'Right, girls, you can start passing these around!'

'I'll just test one,' Carrie announced, taking a bite of sausage. 'Whoo! It's hot!' she said, frantically fanning her mouth. 'But really good!'

'I'm glad they've got the seal of approval,' Mrs Grace laughed, putting more sausages on to the barbecue. 'Don't forget to leave some for the others.'

'Food's up!' Jenny called. 'Is anybody hungry?'

She didn't have to repeat the question. Matt and Vicky handed out paper plates and everyone started to help themselves from the table. Some of Jenny's school friends helped to pass round cans of coke and other drinks as well as bowls of crisps and popcorn. Soon the barbecue was crowded with people laughing, talking and eating.

Mrs Grace was kept busy refilling the platters and, after the first rush, Jenny and Carrie managed to fill a plate for themselves.

'These are yummy!' Jenny congratulated Mrs Turner as she took a bite of her toffee apple.

'They're certainly going down well,' Carrie's mum agreed as young Paul McLay ran up to them, a toffee apple clutched in each hand.

'One of these is for Mum,' he explained breathlessly. 'She's just coming now.'

'Hello, everyone! Sorry I'm late.' Anna McLay, Paul's mother, made her way over to them. 'Well, this looks delicious,' she said, as she took the toffee apple her son offered her.

'Matt, your dad says it's time to start the fireworks,' Ian called over.

'Right!' Matt replied. 'What are we waiting for?' Taking Vicky's hand, he led her over to help.

Jenny watched as Matt and Vicky set off with Ian towards the corner of the field. Fraser had insisted that the fireworks be kept at a safe distance from the spectators.

'It was really good of you to ask us all to the party,' Anna McLay said to Jenny, who was helping Mrs Grace to put potatoes wrapped in tinfoil around the edges of the barbecue.

'Oh, that's OK,' Jenny said as she picked up another potato. 'I met Fiona this morning. She told me she didn't want to come,' she added.

Anna McLay looked embarrassed. 'Well, she had lots of schoolwork she had to finish,' she said lamely. 'And Calum is very busy at the moment, too . . .' Her voice trailed off.

Jenny guessed that, like Fiona, Calum McLay had refused to come to Windy Hill. It seemed that there was just too much bad history between Fraser Miles and Calum McLay for the two men ever to be friends.

'Maybe Fiona will come later when she sees the fireworks,' Ellen said, as a shower of sparks from the bonfire lit up the night and the people nearest to it backed away.

'I don't think so,' Mrs McLay said sadly. 'Fiona has been really difficult recently. I think she's been feeling a bit left out. Paul's operation was such a great success that maybe we made too much fuss of him and neglected Fiona a little. I am trying hard to make it up to her, but it isn't easy.'

Jenny and Carrie, who were listening, looked

at each other. 'No wonder Mrs McLay is having a hard time,' Carrie said to Jenny softly. 'Fiona is bad enough normally. She must be a real misery when she sulks.'

Jenny nodded, her eyes on Paul as he danced round the bonfire, his face alight with laughter. 'Paul is so different,' she said to Carrie. 'He's always cheerful – just like his mum.'

Jenny smiled at Paul who was waving a sparkler in the air. It left trails of light in the darkness. Suddenly there was a great whoosh from the bonfire and a shower of sparks burst upwards.

'Look! The guy's going up!' Carrie called.

Jenny watched as the straw-stuffed guy blazed like a beacon. For a few moments it seemed to come to life, its arms waving in the flames. Then, at the top end of the field a Catherine wheel began to whirl, sending out showers of light. Fraser had started the firework display!

Paul whooped with delight and Jenny watched as Mrs McLay moved towards her son. 'I thought Fiona had changed after Paul nearly drowned,' Jenny said to Carrie and Ellen. 'She seemed so sorry about frightening Paul into running away. It seemed like she'd turned over a new leaf. But then she was really mean to Jess this morning. She threw a stick at him.'

'If you ask me, Fiona will never change,' Carrie sniffed.

Jenny sighed. She had to agree but she wasn't going to worry about sulky Fiona McLay tonight. Tonight she was going to concentrate on enjoying herself. She and Carrie walked over to the crowd round the bonfire. A brilliant shower of sparks burst in the night sky, bathing the whole scene in its light. A rocket followed and another until the sky seemed filled with whistling fireworks exploding in the darkness.

As everyone ooh-ed and aah-ed, Jenny noticed that up on the hill, Darktarn Keep was illuminated, its broken walls looking even more dramatic than usual as coloured lights exploded all over the sky.

'Wow! Look at that one, Mum!' Paul cried, as a huge rocket burst open, showering the surrounding countryside in brilliant red and green stars.

Jenny grinned then turned to Carrie. 'I'm going to take some sausages down to Jess now,' she said. 'Do you want to come?'

Carrie shook her head. 'No, I think I'll stay here to see the last of the fireworks.'

Jess threw himself at Jenny as soon as she opened the kitchen door. He licked her face ecstatically and the only way she got him to stop was by producing the sausages. She watched him gobble up four in a row and laughed. 'Honestly, Jess,' she scolded him. 'Anyone would think I never fed you.'

Jess looked at her, his head on one side and his big dark eyes pleading.

'No,' Jenny said firmly as he butted the pocket of her jacket. 'Those are for Jake and Nell.' Jenny had wrapped some more sausages in foil and put them in her pocket, out of sight. Trust Jess to sniff them out.

Jenny stayed with him for a while, concerned in case the sound of the fireworks was upsetting him. But he seemed fine. From inside the house you could hardly hear the distant explosions and the curtains were safely drawn against the bright lights from the hill.

'I've got to go now, Jess,' she told him at last.

'I've got to check on Mercury and Jake and Nell.'

Jess whined as Jenny backed out of the door and closed it firmly behind her. Jenny made her way across the farmyard and pushed open the stable door. It felt warm and snug in the stables. Mercury whickered softly and the two sheepdogs trotted towards her, tails wagging. Jenny bent to fondle them.

'Good dogs,' she said softly, as Jake and Nell rubbed themselves against her legs. She stroked their rough coats then produced the treats she had brought for them, watching happily as they gobbled up the sausages, licking their lips afterwards and looking for more.

'That's all,' she told them, making her way to Mercury's box. She pulled an apple out of her pocket and held it out on the palm of her hand. The big black horse nuzzled at her hand as he took the apple from it. Jenny reached up her other hand and stroked his mane while Jake and Nell settled down once more.

'You aren't frightened, are you, Mercury?' she whispered.

Mercury whinnied and Jenny put an arm

round his neck. He felt warm and seemed perfectly calm. Jenny listened. She could hear only dull thuds as the fireworks exploded far away up the hill. The animals would be perfectly safe.

Jenny gave the sheepdogs a quick pat then opened the stable door. The night air blew in, cold and clear. She shut the door gently behind her.

As she was crossing the farmyard a rocket lit up the sky and Jenny increased her pace and turned for the top field. It was time she got back to her friends.

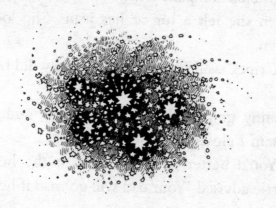

3

'That's the last firework,' Paul sighed, as a golden starburst exploded in the sky.

Jenny sighed too. 'Dad saved the best one until last,' she said.

'Brilliant!' Carrie chimed in, her face still bathed in the glow from the showering sparks.

All around them, friends and neighbours were cheering and clapping. Matt, Ian and Fraser appeared and jokingly took a bow to the assembled company. Jenny was applauding them when she felt a tug at her jeans. She looked down.

'Cripes!' said Carrie. 'It's Jess! How did he get out?'

Jenny gulped. 'I don't know,' she said. 'I'm certain I closed the door after me.'

'You'd better get him back to the house,' Carrie advised. 'Your dad will go mad if he sees Jess.'

Jenny nodded. 'I'll take him back right away,' she said, taking hold of his collar. But Jess kept on tugging, looking up at her intently. 'There's something wrong with him,' Jenny said. 'He won't stop pulling at me.'

'You're right,' Carrie agreed. 'He seems to want to move faster.'

Jess pulled forward again, almost pulling her off balance. Jenny put a hand on the dog's head but he wouldn't be distracted. He *was* acting oddly. Something was wrong.

'I don't know what's got into him,' Jenny said, puzzled.

'I'd better come with you,' Carrie said briskly.

The girls slipped away as quietly as they could.

Jess ran in front of them, turning every so often to urge them on. They were halfway across the field, out of the range of the bonfire's light, when a dark shadow raced up to them.

Jenny swung her torch and switched it on. 'Ian!' she exclaimed.

'Why are you leaving?' Ian asked as Jess scampered back to them. He looked down. 'And what's Jess doing here?'

'He got out somehow,' Jenny explained hurriedly. 'He came to fetch me. We're just going to check that everything is OK down there.'

'I'll come too,' Ian said at once. 'OK, Jess, lead the way!'

At once Jess was off like the wind, skimming across the short-cropped grass, vanishing into the darkness. Jenny swung her torch beam wide, lighting the way in front of them. Jess leapt up on the drystone wall that bordered the field and turned back to them, barking urgently.

'We're coming, Jess,' Jenny gasped as they sped over the field towards the farm. 'What *is* the matter with you?'

Jess was moving faster than ever now, running like the wind towards the farmhouse. Jenny cast a quick look at Ian and Carrie. They were out of breath too, but they carried on, pelting after the young sheepdog, into the farmyard. Jess stood in the middle of the cobbled yard, barking furiously.

Ian sniffed. 'I smell smoke,' he said, urgently.

They stood for a moment, looking round.

Jenny looked up at the first floor of the farmhouse. 'That's odd,' she said. 'I don't remember leaving my bedroom window open.' Then her breath caught in her throat. Smoke was drifting out of her bedroom window, and a flickering orange glow was coming from inside the room. 'Oh, no!' she cried, pointing. 'The farmhouse is on fire!'

Suddenly one of the curtains burst into flames and flapped in the wind, blazing. Bits of burning material drifted across the farmyard. Jenny's eyes went to the stables. There was a scattering of straw on the ground at the base of the stable door. A burning fragment settled on to the straw and it caught alight. A small trail of flames worked its way along the straw and under the gap at the bottom of door, into the stables.

Jenny swung round. Ian was already halfway

across the yard. 'I'll go and fetch help!' he yelled. 'I'll be as fast as I can!'

Jenny nodded. 'I'll see to the animals!' she shouted back. 'We've got to get them out.'

'I'll help you,' Carrie called, following Jenny towards the stables. The straw on the ground was well alight now.

Jenny kicked the burning straw away and wrenched open the stable doors, but it was too late – the fire was already spreading inside. 'Come on, Carrie, we've got to work fast!' she yelled, coughing as a cloud of smoke hit her face. The wood shavings that littered the floor of the stables caught alight as the wind came through the door, fanning the flames. In the far corner Jenny could see flames beginning to lick round a loosebox door.

Just then, two black and white shapes came out through the open doorway and threw themselves on to the cobbled courtyard, panting in the cool night air. It was Jake and Nell. Jenny breathed a sigh of relief, but Jess sniffed round them worriedly.

'They've probably inhaled some smoke,' Carrie said. 'But they're safe now.'

Jenny could hear Mercury whickering nervously in his stall. Suddenly a line of fire raced along the top of a loosebox and burst into flames as it met a rack of hay. There was a terrified whinnying sound. 'Mercury!' Jenny cried. 'Hold on,' she gasped, 'I'm coming!'

Jenny drew her scarf up over her mouth and nose. 'Hang on to Jess out here, Carrie,' she said. 'I might need you to guide me out.'

She went into the stables. Dense smoke billowed round her. Her breath caught in her throat, choking her. Desperately fumbling her way over to Mercury's stall, Jenny tugged at the door. For a horrifying moment she thought the door had jammed. Inside, the big black horse neighed, kicking the walls and rolling his eyes in terror.

Jenny's eyes were smarting so much from the smoke that tears were running down her cheeks, making it virtually impossible to see. As the door opened, she immediately reached in and fumbled for the rope that tethered Mercury. It seemed like an age before it came loose and she was able to get the terrified horse out of the stall.

'Jenny, hurry!' Carrie called, anxiously. 'The doorway's going to catch fire!'

Jenny turned to see flames flickering near the door of the stable. Her way out would be cut off any second. Willing Mercury to keep calm, Jenny urged the terrified horse towards the exit. Mercury tossed his head in panic as flames found their way across the floor of the stable. Jenny's breath rasped in her throat and she felt her own panic rising. The smoke made it almost impossible to concentrate. She dragged the scarf back up over her face but it didn't make her breathing any easier.

Then Jenny became aware of a furious barking. 'Jess!' she cried out. At once, Jess was by her side. The collie pulled at her coat, then ran round to the other side of Mercury, urging him along, reassuring the nervous horse, as he had done on other occasions. Jenny realised that Jess was crouching low. Of course! Nearer the ground the air was fresher and clearer. Clever Jess! Jenny crouched low and immediately found it easier to breathe.

Mercury tossed his head again, then haltingly, followed Jess through the doorway and out to safety. At last Jenny emerged into the open, coughing and choking. Carrie caught her as she stumbled, supporting her while she pulled down her scarf from her face and dragged in great lungfuls of cool, fresh air.

As Jenny recovered, she looked up at her friend, and her heart sank as she saw the dismayed expression on Carrie's face. 'What is it?' she asked.

'The new lambing barn,' Carrie told her. 'It's caught fire.'

Jenny wheeled round to see for herself. 'The ewes are in there,' she cried, her voice hoarse with smoke. 'We have to get them out!'

'No you don't,' a familiar voice said and she found herself in her father's arms.

Jenny looked up at him through eyes smarting with tears. 'Dad! The ewes,' she croaked.

Her father strode across the yard, holding her tightly to his side. 'You're more important than the ewes,' he said, looking anxiously down at her. 'You need to get some more air into those lungs.'

Fraser Miles led Jenny to the far side of the yard and sat her gently down, her back propped against the wall of the farmyard. Jenny's eyes were still streaming but her breathing was getting easier.

Mrs Grace hurried towards them, and bent towards Jenny. 'I'll look after her, Fraser,' she said. 'You'd better try and get those ewes out.'

Fraser nodded, then looked back down at Jenny. 'Are you sure you're all right?' he asked.

Jenny smiled up at him weakly. 'I'm feeling much better already, Dad,' she assured him. 'Now, go!' she urged him. Then she started to cough again.

'Don't try to talk, lass,' Mrs Grace advised her. 'Just breathe deeply.'

Jenny did as she was told. She watched her father run towards the lambing barn. The roof was already well alight and more sparks were drifting on the wind from the burning house all the time. The stone walls of the stables would withstand the fire better than the barn's wooden ones. Matt was there already and the yard seemed to be full of people now. Surely there was a hope that they could save Windy Hill.

Carrie and Ian appeared and crouched down beside her.

'How are you feeling?' Ian asked.

'Fine,' Jenny croaked.

Carrie smiled. 'Liar,' she joked but her face was strained and worried looking.

Jenny tried to smile. Nell was standing beside Ian. The sheepdog shook her head and licked Jenny's hand.

'Nell seems all right now,' Carrie said.

Jenny clutched Carrie's arm. 'Where's Jess?' she asked anxiously.

'He's right here,' Mrs Grace assured her, leading Jess over. 'You just needed a moment to recover.'

'Oh, Jess,' Jenny cried as Jess rushed up to her, licking her face. She put her arms round his neck. 'You got us out of there,' she said softly. 'You're the best dog in the world, Jess.'

Ian looked across at the lambing barn. 'Your dad and Matt are starting to release the ewes now,' he told Jenny. 'I just hope they've got time.'

Jenny nodded. She and Ian both knew that it wasn't a good idea to let all the ewes out at once. They would panic and stampede and the weaker ones would get trampled. They watched as Fraser, Matt and several neighbours began to herd the sheep out of the barn.

Mr Turner had uncoiled the high-pressure hose her father used for cleaning the cobbled farmyard from its wheel on the wall and, as Jenny watched, he turned the tap and pointed the hose at the stables. A great whoosh of water flooded out of the hose, creating billows of steam as the jet sprayed the burning stalls. Then he shifted position and began to douse the roof of the lambing barn.

Jenny looked towards the house. The upstairs was glowing red now; the flames were really taking hold.

'What about the house?' Jenny asked. 'Why doesn't he spray the house?'

'Because there are still animals in the lambing barn,' said Ian. 'They know what they're doing, Jenny.'

Jenny watched the sparks drifting on the air towards the lambing barn and nodded. The house would have to wait. The animals were more important. Jenny could see her father and Matt working frantically to herd the sheep out of the barn. The yard was a confusion of noise as the terrified animals tried to get away from the smell and heat of the burning lambing barn, making Fraser and Matt's job even more difficult.

Vicky and Carrie raced across the farmyard and began to help, guiding the panicking ewes towards the gate at the bottom of the yard. Jake seemed to be everywhere, running between the ewes, forcing them to move in the right direction.

As Matt drove the last of the ewes from the barn, there was a tremendous cracking sound. Jenny watched in horror as the roof creaked, and sagged, threatening to collapse.

'Get out of there, Dad!' Matt yelled. 'Now!'

Jenny saw her father drag one last terrified ewe out of the barn. Then, as if in slow motion, the roof fell in on itself. The fresh wood of the lambing barn, newly primed and painted, had no resistance to the flames. It exploded as the fire hit it. With a great tearing sound the rafters collapsed and Jenny lifted her arms to her face to ward off the heat.

Matt, Vicky and Carrie had the sheep rounded up hard against the far gate, ready to drive them into the lower field. Jenny looked all around her.

The fire was raging through the farmhouse and outbuildings too. Only the shearing shed with its corrugated iron roof seemed to be escaping the flames. A sob tore at her throat as she saw everything she loved go up in the blaze.

'At least they got the sheep out,' Ian said, trying to comfort her.

Mrs Grace put an arm round Jenny's shoulder. 'That's right,' she said. 'After all, the pregnant ewes are Windy Hill's future. That's what's important. And the shearing shed should be all right.'

Jenny turned to Mrs Grace. She knew the housekeeper was only trying to comfort her. 'But look at it,' she cried, the tears coursing down her cheeks. 'Windy Hill is ruined!'

4

'Come on,' Ian said. 'Let's go and see if we can help – if you feel up to it.'

Jenny watched as her father organised a human chain. She saw the silhouettes of all their friends, dark against the blaze beyond them. They were passing buckets from hand to hand. Fraser Miles was encouraging them, directing their efforts where they were most needed.

She dashed her tears away. 'Of course I do,' she said, as she started to follow Ian across the yard.

Mrs Grace laid a hand on her arm. 'Why don't you try to get the sheep into the field?' she said. 'If they stampede we could have an even worse situation on our hands.'

Jenny nodded and turned to Jess. 'Here, boy,' she said. 'We've got work to do.' She looked at Jake and Nell. 'You too,' she said.

All three collies came to heel immediately. Jenny called over to her father. 'We'll get the sheep into the field, Dad,' she told him.

Fraser gave her a critical look. 'You all right?' he asked.

Jenny nodded. Fraser turned to Matt. 'Come on, Matt,' he called. 'We've got to keep the fire at bay until the fire brigade arrives.'

Jenny whirled round as Matt and her father got back to work. 'The fire brigade!' she shouted to them. 'Where are they?'

'We got them on the mobile phone,' Matt said. 'But it's bonfire night, the busiest night of the year for them. It could take them an hour or more to get here. We have to do what we can ourselves to save our home.'

Vicky and Carrie came over. 'Let's get these sheep sorted out, shall we?' Carrie said. Jenny nodded.

'I'll take Mercury out of the way, first,' Vicky said. 'I'll be back as soon as I can to help with the sheep.'

Jenny pushed open the gate. With Ian and Carrie's help she began herding the sheep through. The three sheepdogs moved as one, circling the ewes, keeping them in line.

It seemed to take a long time to get the terrified animals out of the yard and on to the track. Vicky had joined them shortly afterwards and was a great help. Jenny could hear the shouts from the farmyard above the anxious bleating of the sheep. Her father's voice came clearly to her as she closed the gate behind her and started off down the track towards the field gate. Jenny knew that if anyone could save Windy Hill, it would be her father.

Afterwards, as the four of them trudged back up the track, Jenny could see that the whole of the upper storey of the house was now on fire. Her father had the farmyard hose trained on it, desperately trying to keep the fire from spreading. Black wisps of smoke were still rising from the stable but the fire there was out. At least the stables would be saved.

Matt ran towards them, his face streaked with smoke and dirt. 'Grab a bucket!' he yelled as he passed, a bucket in each hand. 'We've got to try and keep the house as wet as possible.'

'Over here,' Vicky called, as she ran for a heap of buckets in the corner of the yard.

Jenny, Ian and Carrie followed her, grabbing a bucket each, dashing back to the standpipe to wait their turn. It seemed a desperately slow process, filling the buckets, passing them on, hoping against hope that they would be able to stem the blaze.

Jenny looked down the line at the row of helpers. Gordon Turner was at the end of the line, directing where the water should be thrown. The fire flickered on faces, blackened by smoke but intent on their work. Jenny heaved her full bucket off the ground and passed it to Ian who was next in line. A small figure ran up behind her.

'Paul!' she cried.

'I'm bringing down the empty buckets,' the little boy told her, then he was off back up the line to wait for the next one.

Jenny swallowed hard and swung the next bucket on down the line. Even little Paul was trying to save Windy Hill.

Half an hour later, her arms aching, and feeling as if she couldn't lift even one more bucket of water, Jenny looked towards the farmhouse. It didn't seem to her as if they were making any difference.

'It isn't any good, is it?' she said to Ian.

Ian shook his head. 'We aren't putting the fire out, if that's what you mean,' he said. 'But we're keeping it at bay. We should be able to salvage stuff from the house and outbuildings even if we can't save the farmhouse.'

Jenny swung her full bucket up the line, suddenly angry. 'Where is the fire brigade?' she cried.

At that moment, she heard the wail of sirens and a cheer went up from the weary line of workers. Fraser Miles turned too but only to encourage them.

'Not long now,' he called, as he held the hose

trained on the upper storey of the farmhouse. 'Just try and hang on.'

As two fire engines rumbled up the track and into the farmyard, the Miles's friends and neighbours set down their buckets one by one. Jenny rubbed her arms as the firemen leaped down from the fire engines.

A fire officer in a white helmet strode across the yard as Fraser handed the hose to Matt and went to meet him. Jenny watched as the firemen, with incredible swiftness, attached their hoses to the tanks on the engines and turned them on. A great arc of water showered down on the burning farmhouse as a line of firemen directed its powerful stream on the building. Then, another group of firemen turned their hose on the lambing barn. The air was filled with the sounds of rushing water and hissing as the flames began to subside beneath the sheer force of water.

Jenny took a deep breath. 'Look at all that water,' she said in wonder. 'That'll put the fire out now.'

'They'll use the water in their tanks until they find another source,' Matt said behind her. 'The

man in the white helmet is the one in charge.'

Jenny watched as Fraser Miles showed the fire officer the standpipe.

'Stand well back, please,' a fire officer in a yellow helmet urged, making his way round the yard.

Obediently everyone dropped back and watched in relief as the firemen worked. Jenny stood against the farmyard wall with Ian and Carrie and the three sheepdogs. Matt was close to them, his arm round Vicky's shoulders. Vicky looked exhausted and Jenny realised that her own knees were weak and throbbing with pain. She slid down the wall and sat with her back to it. Jess snuggled close to her and licked her hand as she settled back against the wall. Carrie and Ian sat down too.

'To think this all started out as the best bonfire night ever,' Carrie sighed. 'What do you think happened?'

Jenny frowned. 'I haven't the faintest idea.'

'The fire could have started in your bedroom,' Ian said. 'Remember, we saw your window wide open and smoke coming from it. The curtains were on fire.'

Jenny shook her head. 'But it couldn't have started there,' she said. 'How could a fire start in my bedroom?'

Fraser Miles came to stand beside them. Mrs Grace was with him. Fraser looked exhausted, his face grey with strain. 'You shouldn't have gone into the stables, Jenny,' he scolded her gently.

'But I had to,' Jenny protested. 'The animals were trapped inside. And anyway, Jess showed me the way out.'

'But you could have been killed, Jenny,' her father insisted.

'Now, now, Fraser,' Mrs Grace said. 'Jenny's had a very upsetting time tonight – we all have. If you're going to give her a telling off, leave it until tomorrow.'

Fraser Miles ran a hand through his hair. 'I suppose I should be grateful you're all right, lass, instead of giving you a row,' he said to her. 'And it was you that raised the alarm. Why did you come down to the farm again? Did you know something was wrong?'

'Not exactly,' said Jenny. 'Jess came and fetched me. He must have smelled the smoke.'

Fraser smiled wearily. 'Jess again,' he said. 'I don't know what we'd do without that dog. Things could have been a lot worse if it hadn't been for him.'

'It's bad enough,' Matt said dismally. 'The stable is gutted. The upstairs of the house is in ruins — and we've lost the lambing barn.'

'Surely the insurance will pay for all the damage?' Mrs Grace said.

Fraser turned to her. His face was streaked with smoke and dirt and he looked utterly weary. 'Aye. They'll pay for the house and the stables,' he said. 'But not for the lambing barn.'

Jenny drew in her breath.

'I hadn't got round to increasing the insurance cover,' Fraser explained. 'I was going to go into Greybridge after the weekend to arrange that. I've had so much on my mind lately. All the profits from the last lambing went into the barn. I might just as well have set fire to the money.'

'You can't blame yourself, Dad,' Jenny protested. 'It isn't your fault. You were going to insure it. Anybody could have forgotten.'

'I shouldn't have forgotten, that's the point, Jenny,' her father said.

Jess rubbed his head against Jenny's legs and she bent to stroke him.

'It'll work out,' Jenny said desperately. 'We've been through bad times before. We've always managed.'

'We always had a place to live before,' Matt said.

'What do you mean?' asked Jenny.

Mrs Grace smiled gently. 'Look around you, Jenny,' she said. 'Windy Hill isn't fit to live in. We're homeless, lass.'

The fires were out now. There were no more flames or smoke, but Jenny could see that the whole place was glistening with the sheen of water. The smell of charred, wet wood filled the air. Mrs Grace was right; nobody would be living at Windy Hill for some time.

'We might have to find somewhere else to live for a while,' Jenny said. 'But we *will* come back to Windy Hill, won't we, Dad?'

Fraser Miles hung his head for a moment. Then he looked up. 'I hope so, Jenny,' he said. 'Right now it isn't looking too good — but I hope so.'

'What's going to happen to us?' Jenny asked.

Fraser Miles straightened up, his face grey with tiredness. 'I'm not quite sure,' he said. 'I'll have to find out what the damage is before we can make any decisions.'

Jenny felt a cold shiver run down her spine. If her dad didn't know what was going to happen to them then things must be bad. She looked across at the farmhouse. The officer in the white helmet was moving towards them. He was carrying a cardboard box.

'The house is safe now,' the chief fire officer said. 'And you should be able to use the stables once you clear them out. It looks as though the fire started in the front bedroom on the east side of the house. We can tell from the extent of the damage and the way a blaze radiates out from the source.'

Fraser looked at Jenny, surprised. 'That's your bedroom, Jenny,' he said.

Jenny frowned. 'I know,' she replied. 'When we first arrived there was smoke coming out of my bedroom window. But I don't remember leaving the window open.'

'I'm taking some materials away with me,' the fire officer told them. 'There was a melted candle and a few burnt out sparklers. Either of those could have started the fire.'

'But I blew my candle out,' Jenny insisted. 'You saw me, Dad.'

'I didn't actually see you blow it out,' Fraser Miles said. 'But I'm sure you did. It isn't like you to be careless.'

'What about the sparklers?' Matt asked.

'But I don't remember taking any sparklers up to my room,' Jenny said, puzzled.

'A fuse blew earlier on tonight,' Matt suggested. 'Could it have been that?'

The fire officer shook his head. 'The blaze started upstairs,' he said. 'The fuse box is downstairs.'

'The thing I want to know,' Ian said, 'is how did Jess get out?'

'What?' said Jenny.

'Look at the window!' Carrie pointed towards the house.

Jenny looked up. Her window gave onto a ledge that ran at an angle down to the porch over the front door. It was a narrow ledge but, if Jess had been desperate, he could have managed to inch his way along out of the window.

'I suppose he could,' Jenny said, puzzled. 'But I was sure I shut him in the kitchen – and, anyway, I *didn't* leave my window open!'

Matt sighed and shook his head. 'Just like you didn't leave a candle burning and you didn't light any sparklers,' he said.

Fraser Miles turned to him. 'That's enough, Matt,' he said. 'We're all upset. Now, leave it!'

Matt laid a hand on Jenny's arm. 'Sorry, Jen,' he said. 'I'm just trying to make sense of all this. *Something* must have happened to start the fire!'

Jenny watched miserably as Matt and Vicky got up and walked across the farmyard. Her father gave her a quick pat on the shoulder and followed them, the fire officer beside him.

Carrie looked across the yard. 'There's Mum. I'd better see what's happening.'

Ian gave Jenny a quick smile. 'You'll feel a lot better tomorrow,' he said as he too walked away.

Jenny watched him cross the yard. She felt as if everyone had abandoned her. Was everyone going to think that the fire had been her fault? A warm, wet tongue licked her hand. She knelt down and cuddled Jess to her.

'It *wasn't* my fault, Jess,' she said. 'You believe me, don't you?'

Jess looked up at her and nuzzled her cheek gently. Jess would always believe in her.

5

Jenny was still kneeling on the cobbles, her arms round Jess's neck, when she felt a hand on her shoulder. She turned to see Carrie standing beside her. Jenny looked up at her friend. 'Oh, Carrie, everyone will think I started the fire,' she said miserably.

Carrie knelt down beside her and gave her a hug. 'Don't worry about that now,' she said. 'Things will look better in the morning –

that's what Mum always says.'

Jenny shook her head. 'It isn't just the fire,' she explained, a tear sliding down her cheek. 'It's the insurance. Dad worked so hard to get the lambing barn and now it's gone and we can't afford to build a new one. Things were going so well, and now we're back where we started.'

Carrie put her hands on Jenny's shoulders. 'Look at me, Jenny,' she said firmly.

Jenny wiped a tear away and looked at her friend.

'Your dad has a lot of worries just now,' Carrie said seriously. 'If he sees that you're so upset he'll just worry even more. You've all got to pull together and try to make the best of things. Your dad isn't angry with you. He loves you, Jenny. Nothing can change that.'

Jenny nodded, unable to speak.

'The best thing we can do is try and sort out the mess. And that means a lot of hard work – starting tomorrow,' Carrie said briskly.

'Tomorrow,' Jenny repeated. 'But where are we going to go tonight?'

'You're coming home with us to Cliff House,' Carrie said. 'Mum's got it all arranged with Mrs

Grace. You're going to share with me. You don't mind, do you?'

Jenny shook her head. 'Jess too?' she asked.

'Especially Jess!' Carrie declared, helping Jenny to her feet.

Jenny gave her a watery smile. 'You're sure your mum won't mind having Jess around?' she asked.

Carrie snorted. 'Jess can't make as much of a mess as I do,' she assured Jenny.

Jenny gave a shaky laugh. 'Thanks, Carrie,' she said as she and Jess followed Carrie across the yard. 'Are we all going to Cliff House?'

Carrie smiled. 'Everybody!' she declared. 'We'll manage – for a while, at least. But we've got Australian relatives coming to stay for Christmas and New Year.'

'Oh, I'm sure everything will be sorted out long before they arrive,' Pam Turner said, bustling up to them.

Jenny looked gratefully at Mrs Turner's smiling face. Carrie's mum was always cheerful and positive.

'I hate the thought of being away from Windy Hill,' Jenny confessed.

'Of course you do,' Pam Turner replied. 'But

you won't be far, and you'll have plenty of opportunities to visit while the repairs are being done. After all, your dad will still have to come over to look after the sheep.' Mrs Turner scratched her shoulder as she thought. 'In fact,' she mused, 'we've got a caravan that Fraser can borrow if he'd rather base himself on site at Windy Hill.'

Carrie hooked her arm around Jenny's. 'Come on,' she said. 'Let's go.'

As they walked away, Jenny looked back one last time at her ruined home. Its walls were black with smoke and the cobbles in the yard were still wet from the fire hoses. The smell of charred wood was everywhere. The lambing barn lay in ruins and some of the upstairs windows of the house were broken. It looked derelict, but Jenny couldn't imagine anywhere else feeling like home for her.

Jenny opened her eyes on Sunday morning and took in unfamiliar white painted walls, blue curtains and the noise of the sea blowing in from the open window. She couldn't work out where she was.

She looked across the room, and there, fast asleep in a nearby bed was Carrie. And then Jenny remembered . . .

The shock and unhappiness of the night before came flooding back. Quietly Jenny got out of bed and went over to the window. She drew the curtains aside and pushed the window further open, leaning out to draw in the fresh sea air. The sea sparkled in the morning sun.

'It's a great view, isn't it?' Carrie said sleepily from the other side of the room.

Jenny turned and smiled at her friend. 'It's wonderful,' she replied.

Carrie sat up in bed, her hair tousled. She yawned. 'But so is the view from your bedroom at Windy Hill.'

Jenny didn't say anything.

Carrie jumped out of bed and came to stand beside Jenny. 'And you'll have that view again, Jenny. Really you will!' she said. 'Come on, let's get dressed and go downstairs.'

Jenny looked at Carrie in dismay. 'But I haven't got any clothes!' she replied. She had borrowed a nightie from Carrie. 'The things I was wearing last night are all in the wash – and

the rest were burned in the fire.'

Carrie darted over to her wardrobe and hauled the door open. 'Take whatever you want!' she said, as a pile of jumpers fell out from the top shelf. 'Oops!' she exclaimed. 'I told you my room was a tip.'

Jenny smiled in spite of herself and picked up a jumper. 'Thanks, Carrie,' she said.

Carrie dragged a pair of jeans off another shelf and handed them to Jenny. 'You'll have to roll the legs up. They'll be a bit big for you.'

Ten minutes later the girls had washed and made their way downstairs. Jess launched himself at Jenny as soon as she opened the kitchen door. He'd slept in the kitchen on a hastily made up bed. Jenny hugged him, feeling better already. 'Jess, you smell of smoke,' she said. 'I'm afraid that means a bath for you later!'

Mrs Grace was in the kitchen, bustling about, getting breakfast ready. She popped a couple of slices of bread in the toaster. 'I told your mother we would share the cooking, Carrie,' she said, smiling. 'I'll do breakfast and lunch and she'll do dinner. Your mum has just popped down to the village and your dad went down to the harbour to do some work on the boat.'

Carrie grinned. 'That's OK with me, Mrs Grace,' she said. 'You're a great cook!'

'Is Dad up yet?' Jenny asked.

Mrs Grace nodded. 'He, Matt and Ian were up early. They've taken Mr Turner's caravan up to Windy Hill. They'll be back in an hour or so.'

'But I wanted to go with them,' Jenny protested.

Mrs Grace shook her head. 'Your dad told me to let you sleep while he gets the caravan sorted out,' she explained. 'He reckons he'll be better off staying at Windy Hill as much as he can. It'll give us all more room here, as well as meaning he can be on the spot to look after the sheep.'

Jenny nodded. 'Matt and Vicky have to go back to college later today,' she said. 'At least we'll have more room then.' She sighed. She knew it was going to be hard on her father without Matt's help.

Carrie took the toast as it popped up and spread the slices thickly with butter and marmalade, handing one to Jenny. 'How about taking Jess for a walk on the beach?' she suggested. 'He always likes that.'

Jenny looked doubtful. 'So long as we're back before Dad,' she said.

'We'll be back,' Carrie promised.

'A walk sounds a good idea,' Mrs Grace put in.

Jenny looked at Jess. The Border collie was already at the kitchen door, waiting. He had recognised the word 'walk'. 'All right,' she said. 'Jess *would* like that.'

'We'll easily be back in an hour,' Jenny promised Mrs Grace.

Ellen Grace nodded. 'You'll get a proper breakfast when you come back,' she said. Jess was out of the door as soon as it was open, speeding ahead.

The girls were heading down the high street in Cliffbay towards the harbour when Carrie pulled on Jenny's arm. 'That's Mr McLay's Land Rover,' she said.

Jenny turned as the Land Rover swept past them and drew up outside the newsagent's. Paul was in the back with Fiona and, as his father got out of the driver's door, the little boy scrambled out of the back and came running towards them with Toby at his heels.

Jenny watched Mr McLay walk into the newsagent's. He was a big man with short dark hair, like Fiona's.

'Jenny!' Paul cried as he reached them. Jess and Toby immediately started chasing each other. Paul seemed to hesitate, then he asked, 'Is Windy Hill going to be all right?'

Jenny smiled at him. 'We hope so, Paul,' she said. 'There's an awful lot of work to be done. We'll have to wait and see what repairs are needed.'

Suddenly the hackles rose on Jess's neck and he growled fiercely. Jenny looked at him in surprise. 'Jess, what on earth's the matter?' She'd never heard him growl quite so fiercely before. Jenny followed Jess's gaze and saw Fiona McLay walking towards them.

'More like rebuilding, I hear,' she said in a mocking voice. As she drew closer, Jess's growling grew louder. Looking at him, Fiona decided to take no chances and stayed a safe distance away. Her pale blue eyes flicked to Jenny, looking her up and down. 'Nice jeans,' she remarked. 'Hand-me-downs, are they? You can't have bought something so nice yourself.'

Jenny flushed. Fiona had always taunted her about not having expensive, fashionable clothes.

But Carrie leaped to Jenny's defence. 'Jenny lost everything in the fire,' she said. 'She borrowed a pair of my jeans. What's wrong with that?'

Fiona shrugged. 'Jenny never cared what she wore anyway so I don't suppose she minds cast-offs,' she sneered.

Jenny shook her hair back from her face. 'No, I don't,' she said to Fiona. 'It was good of Carrie to lend them to me. I didn't have anything else to wear.'

'You shouldn't have been so careless then, should you?' said Fiona.

Jenny gasped. 'What do you mean?' she asked.

Fiona shrugged. 'Everyone's talking about it,' she said. 'We all know how the fire started – that *you* burned down your precious Windy Hill.' Fiona's eyes narrowed. 'So how do you feel about that, Jenny Miles?' she challenged.

'But it's not true!' Jenny protested.

Carrie took a step towards Fiona but Jess was ahead of her. Placing himself between Jenny and

Fiona, he stood there stiffly, growling up at the other girl.

Fiona stepped back quickly as Jess gave a sharp bark and moved towards her. 'Call that dog off!' she cried in a rising voice. 'He's going to bite me!'

'Jess wouldn't bite anybody,' Jenny said.

Fiona looked at her, her face flushed. 'Yeah, and you don't start fires, do you?' she said, then she turned on her heel and marched off back to her father's Land Rover.

Jess stood there, still growling softly and Jenny bent to reassure him. She stroked him gently until he began to calm down. 'Well!' she said, turning to Carrie. 'What was *that* all about? I've never seen Jess behave like that before!'

Carrie shook her head. 'I don't know, but he certainly seems to have something against Fiona – though goodness knows what!'

Jenny looked up at her. 'Do you think what she said is true? Does everyone think it was my fault?'

Paul laid a hand on her arm. 'I don't, Jenny,' he said. 'I don't care what anybody says. I don't believe it.'

Jenny felt tears prick the back of her eyes. 'Thanks, Paul,' she said softly. But it was clear that the rumours were spreading already.

'Paul!' Mr McLay called as he came out of the newsagent's.

Jenny looked up.

Calum McLay took a few steps towards her. 'Oh, it's you,' he said to Jenny. 'I heard you lost your home,' he said shortly.

He led Paul away, back to the Land Rover. But before he got in he turned back to look at Jenny. 'You ought to be more careful, you know,' he said. 'Starting fires is a serious business.'

Jenny watched dumbly as the Land Rover started up and drove away. It was true then. The whole of Graston and Cliffbay thought the fire was her fault. She had been so sure she had put out that candle . . .

'Jenny,' Carrie said gently, 'let's take Jess down to the beach.'

Jenny swallowed hard and nodded.

6

Later that day, after the firemen had declared it safe, Jenny and her family returned to Windy Hill to help clear up and salvage what hadn't been ruined in the fire. It was like re-visiting a nightmare. Her bedroom was a charred shell. The bright yellow walls were now black and smeared with soot and water. The remains of the curtains hung like limp, black rags at the window. And everywhere there was the choking smell of burning.

Jenny recognised her bookcase amongst the debris and felt a lump in her throat as she looked at the sodden, burned remains of all her favourite books. She had kept all of the picture books that her mother had read to her when she was little and now they were gone. She remembered how she and her mother had painted the little bookcase together a few years ago.

As Jenny sifted through the remains, a subdued Jess staying close by her side, she remembered an even more precious, irreplaceable item, that had now been lost for ever: the photograph of her mother as the Graston Lass that she'd kept on her bedside table. Jenny's eyes filled with hot tears. So much of her life had gone up in flames.

She felt Jess lick her hand reassuringly and looked down at him. 'It's OK, boy,' she said. 'I know. We've still got the most important thing – each other.'

Jenny heard footsteps coming towards the bedroom. Carrie had turned up to help as well. Ian followed her into the room carrying a box of sodden blackened clothes and books. He dumped it down on the floor and looked around. 'Goodness, Jen,' he said. 'There isn't much left to salvage here, is there?' he said sympathetically.

Jenny shook her head and turned away.

Carrie came over and gave her a hug. 'I know it's terrible, Jenny, but we've got to look on the bright side. Just think! As soon as the insurance money has been paid out, we can go and choose you a whole new wardrobe. It'll be great fun!'

Jenny smiled. She could tell that Carrie was just as shocked by the charred, ruined room, but was trying hard to be cheerful for her sake.

Jenny pointed to her desk. It was blackened and scorched, the books and project work on top of it now a pile of ashes.

'Oh, the Geography project,' Carrie dismissed. 'Don't worry about that. You can share mine!'

'We could do a new one together if you like,' Ian offered. 'My bedroom escaped the fire but my project work got soaked. It's ruined. There's a lot of water damage from the fire hoses.'

Jenny nodded, then walked over to the charred bedroom doorway. 'Come on, let's go and see what's happening outside.'

With Jess running ahead, Jenny, Carrie and Ian went downstairs and out into the farmyard.

There was no shortage of helpers today, Jenny noticed. Many of the people who had been at the bonfire party had turned out to lend a hand with the salvage operation.

Gordon Turner was helping Fraser in the stables, clearing out the debris. The caravan Fraser planned to stay in was parked at the far end of the farmyard.

It would be strange to have her father living here amongst the ruins of Windy Hill while she was at Cliff House, Jenny thought. But she could see the sense in it. He would want to be on the spot, not just for the animals' sake, but to oversee the repairs to the buildings.

'Mercury should be OK in the less damaged end of the stables now,' Matt said, as he passed with a barrowload of blackened wood and tipped it on to the growing pile in the middle of the yard. Mercury had had to spend the previous night in an adjoining field. 'And once they've been cleaned out, we'll be able to use the other end to house some of the ewes, if need be.'

Jenny looked up at her bedroom window. She was still mystified as to how the fire could have started in there. She didn't hear her father approach.

'We'll be able to replace most of what you've lost in time, lass,' he said. 'Now, I'm going up to take a look at the breeding ewes. Mr Turner is finishing up in the stables and Mrs Grace is going through the kitchen, trying to salvage as much as she can. If anyone comes about the insurance I'll be back in an hour.'

Jenny nodded but as Fraser walked away, a tear slid down her cheek.

'What is it, Jenny?' Ian asked.

Jenny looked at him. 'What if I really didn't blow that candle out properly? What if it *was* my fault? I'm so confused now that I can't be sure any longer.'

'It must be so hard for you,' Carrie said sympathetically. 'But whatever happened, it was an accident. You can't blame yourself, Jenny.'

Jenny dashed away the tears, impatient with herself. 'It's just that there are some things that can never be replaced,' she answered. 'Like the photograph of Mum I kept on my bedside table – and Mrs Turner's sketch of Jess as a puppy.'

Ian put his hand on her arm. 'Come on,' he

said. 'There's a pile of stuff over here that escaped the fire. Let's go through it. You never know what you might find.'

'Jess has made a start on it already,' Carrie said. 'Look at him!'

Jess had scampered across to the pile of debris in the corner of the yard and was snuffling at it.

'OK,' said Jenny, forcing a smile. 'We might as well give him a hand.'

Jenny and Carrie followed Ian to the corner of the yard and began to sort through the pile. Jess was rooting around, sniffing furiously and dragging out bits and pieces for their inspection.

'Oh, look,' said Jenny, delighted. 'You've found your feeding bowl, Jess. Good boy!'

Jess wagged his tail hard and started rooting in the pile again. This time he came up with his old blue blanket and brought it proudly over to Jenny. Jenny took it from him gently. It was wet and dirty and smelled of smoke but to Jenny it looked beautiful. This was the blanket she had wrapped Jess in just after he was born. 'Oh, Jess,' she said softly. 'I'm so glad you found this. I'll wash it for you and it'll be as good as new. It'll make you feel at home

while we're living at Cliff House.'

Jess licked her cheek and Jenny smiled. Maybe they would find other treasures too.

An hour later Jenny stood up and stretched her arms above her head, loosening out her aching back. A small heap of objects lay to one side, the result of sifting through the salvage pile. There was a book that she'd left on an arm of the sofa downstairs, a bit smoky but still readable. And her new jacket that had been in the downstairs cloakroom.

There was also a pile of sports equipment – tennis racquet, roller skates and her hockey stick, which had been in the cupboard under the stairs.

'Well, at least you'll be able to play in the school hockey team,' Carrie grinned.

Jenny grinned back, feeling better. 'Just look at the state of us!' she said. They were grimy with soot.

'Looks like we've got a visitor,' Ian announced, turning round.

Jenny turned to see a car drawing into the farmyard. A youngish woman got out. Jenny looked at the woman with interest. She was wearing a smart bright blue suit and high-heeled shoes – not the sort of clothes people usually wore when they came to visit a farm.

'Who's that?' said Carrie, straightening up.

'Dad was expecting someone from the insurance company,' Jenny said. 'I suppose that's her.'

The woman looked around the yard and, as her eyes fell on Jenny, Carrie and Ian, she began to walk towards them.

'Hello, I'm Marion Stewart,' the woman said in a bright voice as she reached them. 'I'm from Capital Insurance and I arranged to meet Mr Fraser Miles here.'

Jenny wiped her right hand on her jeans and held it out. 'I'm Jenny Miles,' she said. 'Fraser Miles is my father. He should be back soon.'

Marion Stewart took a quick look at Jenny's grubby hand and pretended she hadn't noticed that Jenny had offered to shake hands. She took a step back. 'I hope he won't keep me waiting. It's inconvenient enough, being called out on a Sunday.'

Carrie and Ian looked at Jenny as the woman turned away towards her car, carefully picking her way through the charred rubble in the yard in her high heels.

'You'd think she'd have realised it would be messy up here, after a fire,' Ian said scornfully.

Carrie giggled. 'Look at Jess,' she said.

The Border collie had unearthed a smoke-blackened cushion from the pile of debris and had decided to present it to Marion Stewart. Jenny watched as Jess scampered in front of the woman and laid his present at her feet.

'Ugh!' said Marion Stewart as the filthy object landed on her highly polished shoes. 'Shoo! Go away, bad dog!'

Jess looked up at her appealingly and licked her hand. She snatched it away. 'Whose dog is this?' she demanded.

'Mine,' said Jenny, trying to keep a straight face. 'He's only trying to be friendly, Miss Stewart. He's brought you a present.'

'Well, I can do without presents like that,' Miss Stewart said sniffily.

Jenny called Jess back. The Border collie picked up his cushion and trotted back to the pile of debris with it. He began rooting around for something else.

Miss Stewart breathed a sigh of relief, then leaned into her car and took out a sheaf of papers from a folder on the passenger seat. 'I shall need a list of all the things you've lost. Do you think you could help with that?'

Jenny nodded. As she began to move towards Miss Stewart's car, Jess laid something at her feet. Jenny looked down, smiling. 'I like your presents, Jess, even if some people don't,' she said, bending to pick up the flat, blackened object. She rubbed a corner of it clean and gasped. It was a photo frame.

'Ian, Carrie!' she breathed. 'It's my photo of Mum. Oh, Jess, you clever thing. You've found the thing that mattered most.' She bent down to give the Border collie a hug. Jess wagged his tail delightedly at the happy tone in Jenny's voice and gave her a sooty lick on the cheek.

Carrie and Ian gathered round to admire Jess's find and Marion Stewart strode back towards them. 'What's that?' she asked. 'I have to make a list of anything you salvage from the fire.' She leaned over and looked down at the photo as Jenny scrubbed its glass front clean with her sleeve.

'It's a photo of my mother when she was the Graston Lass,' Jenny explained. Every year in Graston, a girl was chosen to be a sort of queen for the day when a spring celebration called the Riding of the Marches took place. The Graston Lass had to ride round the town at the head of a procession. It was a great honour and Jenny had been chosen as Graston Lass herself the previous spring. What was more, Mrs Grace had remembered that she had an old photograph of Sheena Miles as the Graston Lass. She'd hunted the photograph out and had given it to Jenny.

Jenny smiled down at the photograph of her mother. 'Mum died in a riding accident the summer before last,' Jenny said, still gazing at the picture.

Marion Stewart tutted. 'I'm sorry to hear that,' she said. Then she looked thoughtful. 'I didn't know your father was a widower. There's no mention of it on our paperwork.'

Jenny smiled bleakly and tucked her treasure safely into the pocket of her jacket. 'He doesn't talk about losing Mum much,' she said. Then she looked up as her father drove into the yard. 'Here he is now.'

Fraser Miles strode across the farmyard and held out his hand to Miss Stewart, his deep blue eyes looking tired, but relieved to see her.

Marion Stewart fixed her eyes on Fraser's face and held out her own hand. Jenny noticed that she didn't even look to see if Fraser's hand was clean.

'How do you do, Mr Miles,' she said. 'I'm Marion Stewart, from Capital Insurance.'

'Hello, Miss Stewart,' Fraser replied. 'I hope I haven't kept you waiting.'

Marion Stewart gave him a dazzling smile. 'Not at all,' she said. 'And please, call me Marion.'

'Do you know what I think?' Carrie said as Mr Miles and Marion Stewart walked off towards the caravan.

'What?' asked Jenny.

'I reckon Miss Stewart has taken a shine to your dad,' Carrie said.

Jenny whirled round. 'What?' she squeaked. 'But she can't have – he's Dad!'

Carrie grinned. 'OK, don't fly off the handle. But she looked very interested in him, to me.'

Jenny frowned as she remembered Marion's change of attitude the moment she met Fraser

Miles. Maybe Carrie was right. Maybe Marion Stewart *had* taken a shine to her father. Jenny wasn't at all sure how she felt about the idea.

'Did the insurance representative come yet?' Mrs Grace asked Jenny, as she came out of the house a while later with a box of soot-smeared crockery.

Ellen Grace's hair was coming down round her face and she had a black streak across one cheek. She was dressed in old jeans and a checked shirt, but it occurred to Jenny that given the choice between a dishevelled Ellen Grace and the smart Miss Stewart, she would rather have Mrs Grace any day.

Jenny nodded. 'They're going over some paperwork in the caravan,' she said. 'But I don't think Miss Stewart likes farms very much – at least she isn't very keen on animals, or mess!'

'Hmm,' Mrs Grace said thoughtfully. 'I hope that won't stop her from appreciating just what a disaster the fire at Windy Hill is for your father. Sheep farming is his whole life.'

Jenny stood up and tucked a hand through

Mrs Grace's arm. 'You understand though, don't you, Mrs Grace?' she said.

'Indeed I do, Jenny,' Ellen Grace replied. 'And I know how important it is to you and Matt too.'

Jenny squeezed Mrs Grace's arm affectionately. 'Jess found the photo of Mum you gave me,' she said. 'It wasn't burnt up in the fire.'

Ellen Grace's face lit up. 'Oh, I'm so glad for you, lass,' she said. 'I know you would have hated to lose that.'

'You're right,' Jenny smiled. 'You know us all so well, Mrs Grace,' she said. 'What would we do without you?'

7

Waking up in Carrie's bedroom wasn't such a shock the next morning, though Jenny resented having to go to school when there was still so much work to be done on the farm. But her father had insisted that her education came first, so, reluctantly, Jenny went off to school with Carrie and Ian.

She was hardly through the school gates before people started coming up to her to ask how she was. The classmates who had been at the bonfire knew about the disaster already, of course, and news had quickly spread throughout the school.

'People are being really kind,' Jenny said to Carrie, after Zoe Burns, one of her classmates, stopped to offer Jenny a personal stereo. 'I know you lost everything,' Zoe had said. 'I got a new one for my birthday so you can have this for as long as you want.'

The good wishes and offers of help flooded in.

'But not everyone is being kind,' Carrie pointed out disapprovingly. 'You should see the look Fiona McLay just gave you. I don't understand why she can't let up, after all you've gone through.'

Jenny looked around and caught Fiona's eye as she crossed the playground. Fiona tried to sidle past the group round Jenny but Amy Jarrow stopped her.

'Oh, Fiona, did you hear about the terrible fire at Windy Hill?' Amy asked.

Fiona stopped and looked challengingly at Jenny. 'You mean the one that Jenny started?' she said.

Amy gasped. 'That's a horrible thing to say,' she exclaimed.

Several of the others were surprised at Fiona's comment. 'You've got no right to go around making accusations like that,' said Mark Armstrong, a friend of Ian's.

Fiona shrugged. 'Believe what you want,' she said, flushing. 'Everyone seems to think that Jenny Miles is an angel – but she isn't. You'll see!' She walked on, then turned back again, a sneer on her lips. 'Anyway, the Mileses are always in trouble. Jenny should be used to it by now. All this fuss about her precious Windy Hill!' she scoffed. 'It's just a little farm.'

Jenny felt herself go pale as Fiona brushed past her. 'Windy Hill is the best sheep farm in the Borders!' she called after her.

'Well, of all the cheek,' Carrie said. 'What a pain in the neck she is! Don't listen to her, Jen.'

Jenny forced herself not to cry. The worst thing she could do was let Fiona see how hurt she was. She shrugged. 'Oh, who cares about Fiona?' she said, as lightly as she could. 'What harm can she do?'

★ ★ ★

Miss Kerr, who was also Jenny's form teacher, called her out before registration and spoke quietly to her.

'I'm all right, really,' Jenny told her. 'No one was hurt and the animals are safe. I suppose that's all that really matters.'

Miss Kerr looked at her sympathetically. 'Just try to concentrate on your work and don't worry too much, Jenny. I'm sure things will work out,' she said.

During their first lesson, Fiona leaned over towards Jenny's desk. 'Did you tell Miss Kerr that you started the fire, Jenny?' she taunted.

Jenny turned to Fiona. 'You seem to be really pleased that Windy Hill burned down, Fiona,' she said, shaking her head. 'Why?'

Carrie had heard Fiona's taunts too. 'Leave off, Fiona,' she hissed. 'If you can't say anything nice, you'd better keep your nasty mouth shut!'

Fiona flushed a deep red.

Catching the disapproving eye of their teacher, the girls turned back to their work.

But Jenny couldn't get over Fiona's apparent satisfaction at the Mileses' misfortune. She turned back to the other girl. 'How can you be like this?' she asked. 'Somebody could have been killed in that fire. There were animals there. Jess was in the house.' Jenny shook her head in disbelief, adding, 'No wonder nobody likes you.'

Fiona flinched and went white.

Jenny bit her lip. Fiona's unkind words had the effect of dragging her down to the same level. 'I'm sorry, Fiona,' she said. 'I shouldn't have said that.'

Fiona looked at her for a long moment. 'But everybody likes *you*, don't they? Little Miss Popular!'

Jenny was amazed to see that Fiona's eyes were shiny with tears. Blinking them away, Fiona turned back to her desk, her cheeks flaming.

Jenny sighed. She didn't think she would ever understand Fiona McLay, but right now she didn't even care to try. Fiona McLay was just plain nasty.

Jenny tried to avoid Fiona as much as possible but on Wednesday she found herself sharing a bench with her for a chemistry lesson. The class were gathered round Miss Eevers, the chemistry teacher, who was demonstrating an experiment.

Picking out a piece of sodium from the glass dish she was holding, the teacher dropped the grey substance into a bowl of water. The sodium began to whizz round the surface of the water, giving off flames.

Everyone craned forward to watch. Amy Jarrow leaned too far over and jogged Miss Eevers's arm. The glass dish in her hand tilted and the rest of the sodium slid into the bowl of water. At once, the flames ignited much higher. Everyone gasped and drew back.

Miss Eevers calmly reached for a fire blanket and dropped it quickly over the flames. Jenny shivered. The flames reminded her of the fire at Windy Hill. Then she heard Fiona's stool scrape back.

'Miss Eevers, can I go to the loo?' Fiona asked.

Miss Eevers nodded abstractedly as she lifted the fire blanket and checked the fire was out.

'What's up with Fiona?' Ian said. 'She looked white as a sheet.'

'Maybe she felt sick,' Carrie suggested. Then she frowned. 'But who cares about her anyway!'

Jenny didn't argue with that. She didn't have any sympathy to waste on Fiona.

★   ★   ★

Fiona didn't return to the chemistry class and she wasn't at school the next day either. Jenny decided she must have been taken ill.

'Has anyone been in touch with Fiona McLay?' Miss Kerr asked, when Fiona had still not returned by the end of the week. 'I was wondering how she was.'

There was silence in the class.

'I see her little brother sometimes,' Jenny offered, eventually. 'I could ask him about her.'

'That would be good of you, Jenny,' Miss Kerr replied.

'Why did you offer to find out how Fiona is?' Carrie asked, as they came out of class. 'She wouldn't do the same for you.'

Jenny shrugged. 'Paul is coming over after school anyway. I'm not going to any trouble.'

Paul, Jenny and Carrie often walked the dogs on the beach at Cliffbay. It was one of Jess's favourite places, and anywhere Jess was, Toby was happy to be there too. Paul's little terrier adored Jess.

'Is Fiona any better?' Jenny asked Paul later that afternoon, as they walked along the beach, throwing sticks for Toby and Jess. The wind blew cold, whipping the waves into white caps. Jenny shivered despite her warm jacket and woolly hat.

'I don't think so,' Paul replied, vaguely.

'What do you mean?' Carrie asked, looking puzzled. 'Can't you tell if she's getting better?'

Paul stopped to pick up the stick Toby had dropped at his feet. 'Well, the thing is, I don't really know what's wrong with her,' he admitted. 'I mean, she hasn't got the measles or anything, I know that. But last night she woke us all up, crying really loudly. It was terrible!' He watched the dogs racing around for a while, then continued. 'She was really upset and wouldn't go back to bed. Mum sat up with her in the living room. She says she keeps having bad dreams.'

'No wonder,' Carrie muttered under her breath. 'Fiona's mind is so nasty, I can't imagine her dreams are any better.' She threw the stick wildly and it landed at the water's edge. A wave rolled in and drew it out into deeper water.

Jenny looked out to sea. Dark clouds were gathering. It looked as if it would be a stormy night. Toby and Jess didn't seem to mind. They were having a wonderful romp along the beach. Jess plunged into the water to retrieve the stick Carrie had thrown, getting to it just before Toby did. The dogs raced back, shaking themselves dry and spattering droplets of freezing cold water all over the place.

'Do you know what the dreams are about?' Jenny asked Paul, as she took a turn to throw the stick.

Paul shrugged. 'She won't tell us. Mum is really worried about her.' He looked up at Jenny. 'It's no fun at home just now,' he said. 'I much prefer being here with you and Jess.'

Jenny grinned at him. It couldn't be easy for Paul, having a sister like Fiona.

'Well, you and Toby can come over to Cliff House whenever you want,' Carrie said. 'Mum won't mind, even if it is a bit crowded at the moment.'

Marion Stewart turned up at Windy Hill that weekend. Jenny, Mrs Grace, Ian and Carrie were in the house, getting stuck into cleaning up the downstairs' walls before they could be redecorated. Though the ground floor rooms hadn't been burned, they'd been ruined by smoke and water damage.

Fraser and Matt were loading sacks of feed into the back of the jeep in the yard when the insurance representative's car turned in at the gate. Fraser went to meet her while Matt heaved another sack into the jeep, ready to transport to the feeding troughs in the fields.

'What does she want now?' Matt said to Jenny, who had taken mugs of tea out to them. 'Dad says she's been to see him twice already this week.'

'There certainly *does* seem to be a lot of paperwork,' Mrs Grace said, as she and Carrie came out into the yard too. She frowned. 'I hope this doesn't mean another hold-up.'

Jenny and Carrie looked at each other. 'I think she just likes coming to see Mr Miles,' Carrie muttered.

Jenny was beginning to think that Carrie was right. Maybe Marion Stewart really *was* making excuses to come and see her father.

But perhaps that wasn't the case at all. When Fraser Miles had finished talking to Miss Stewart and seen her off, he came over to them, looking worried.

'What is it, Dad?' Jenny asked, as her father started loading sacks into the jeep.

'Marion says she'll need to make a few more visits before she can put in her report,' Fraser Miles replied. 'Her boss is being a bit sticky about the claim. I'll try and get in to see him myself on Monday.' He stopped and rubbed his eyes wearily. 'I had hoped the repairs would be under way by now.'

Jenny looked at her father. He looked tired. It wasn't easy clearing up the aftermath of the fire and looking after the flock at the same time. He swung another sack into the back of the jeep and climbed into the driver's seat. 'Ready, Matt?' he asked.

Matt got in and they drove away.

'It'll work out,' Carrie said, putting her arm round Jenny's shoulder.

Jenny looked at her. 'But when?' she asked. 'We can't stay with you at Cliff House forever.'

The subject came up again the following evening, when they were all sitting round the big kitchen table at Cliff House. Outside, the wind was howling and the moon shone brightly on the storm-tossed sea.

Matt had gone back to college, promising to return the following weekend. On the two nights he was home he would share the caravan with his father. Cliff House was big enough to accommodate Jenny, Ian and Mrs Grace, but putting Matt up too would stretch things to the limit.

'I'd thought we'd be well on the way towards making Windy Hill habitable by now,' Fraser said. 'But while the insurance company delays paying out for the work that needs to be done, we're not getting anywhere.'

'When will Marion be able to give permission for the repairs to get started?' Mrs Grace asked. 'We can't stay here indefinitely – no matter how welcome we are.'

Pam Turner smiled. 'I'm afraid that's true,' she said. 'We've got our Australian relatives coming at the beginning of next month and I've promised to put them up.'

Jenny looked closely at her father. He still looked exhausted. Deep lines were etched around his mouth. He had to work all the daylight hours just to keep things ticking over at Windy Hill.

'I've been in touch with the builders,' Fraser replied. 'They'll be ready to start just as soon as they get the go-ahead from Marion. Let's hope that doesn't take too much longer.'

But by the following weekend the insurance company still hadn't paid up. Fraser was beside himself with frustration and worry. And the weather had taken a turn for the worse. It had been a stormy week and there was a stiff breeze coming off the sea.

Jenny, Ian and Carrie were helping Matt to fix pens in the stables so that Fraser could winter the weaker ewes under shelter. At least with the stables and the shearing shed still in use, Windy Hill would be all right as far as the sheep were concerned.

Jenny went to the door of the stables and looked at the clouds massing on the horizon. 'Do those look like rain clouds to you?' she asked Carrie.

Carrie pulled her woolly hat further

down over her ears and shivered. 'Dad said this morning that he thought it would snow before long,' she said.

'Let's hope your dad can get the work on the house started before winter really sets in,' Ian put in. 'If we get a really bad winter it could be spring before the repairs get underway.'

Jenny sighed. *And where would we live until then?* she thought worriedly.

Just then, Fraser Miles called a halt for lunch. They were tucking into sandwiches and bowls of soup that Mrs Grace had heated on the caravan's gas cooker when Marion Stewart arrived again.

'Let's hope there's some good news for a change,' Fraser said, as he went to meet her car.

He brought the insurance representative into the crowded little caravan, saying, 'Surely you can authorise the repairs now? If we don't get started on the repair work before the winter sets in, we'll be stranded! Surely Bob Elliot must realise that.'

Jenny had heard Bob Elliot's name mentioned before. He was Marion Stewart's boss at the insurance company.

Miss Stewart looked sympathetic. 'I'm sorry, Fraser,' she apologised. 'I'm doing my best but Bob is dragging his heels. I'm not sure why. I submitted my damage report almost two weeks ago, as you know. But when I chased him about it again this morning, he made some excuse about needing to check some details – and that was the last I heard of it. Then he rushed out to lunch with that neighbour of yours.'

Fraser looked at her narrowly. 'Neighbour?' he repeated.

Marion Stewart nodded. 'Someone called Calum McLay,' she said. 'I know, because Mr McLay left a message with me confirming that he could make their lunch date.'

At the mention of Calum McLay's name Fraser turned white. 'What details need to be checked?' he asked, tightly. Jenny could see that her father was having a hard time keeping his temper.

Marion shrugged. 'I really couldn't say,' she replied. 'We know that the fire started in Jenny's bedroom,' she said, giving Jenny a look. 'And that it was probably caused by a lighted candle falling over, which makes it an accident.' Jenny felt herself flushing as the woman went on talking. 'So, as I've reported on the cause and the damage, I really don't understand this delay.' She shook her head. 'I've never known Bob to be this slow about a claim.'

Jenny looked at her father again. 'I don't think it's a coincidence that Bob Elliot is having lunch with Calum McLay today,' Fraser said seriously. 'Thank you, Marion. I think I know what's going on here now.'

Marion looked puzzled but Fraser wouldn't say any more about it. Jenny decided to ask her father what he meant after Marion had gone.

'Do you think Mr McLay has got something to do with the delay?' she asked, as soon as Marion's car disappeared down the track.

Fraser nodded. 'Yes, I do.'

'But why would he want to interfere?' Jenny asked.

Her father shrugged. 'Maybe he thinks that if I have to wait long enough for the insurance money, I won't be able to keep Windy Hill running. Maybe he's still hoping to force me to sell up to him.'

'It could be even worse, Dad,' Matt said

worriedly. 'If Mr McLay really wants to cause trouble, he might try to persuade the insurance company that the fire was our fault . . .' Jenny caught him looking at her, and he looked away again, embarrassed. 'Then they might not pay out at all,' he finished.

Jenny's heart sank. She had always thought that losing Windy Hill would be the worst thing in the world. But if everyone thought that she was to blame, that would be even worse.

'Dad,' she said. 'I know they say the fire started in my room but, honestly, I blew that candle out – I'm sure I did.'

Fraser shook his head. 'Whatever happened with the candle can't be changed, lass,' he said sadly. 'The important thing now is to get the repairs started.'

'Maybe it was a spark from the bonfire,' Jenny said desperately.

'Look, let's stop pretending, Jenny,' Matt said impatiently. 'You know it wasn't.' He stopped when he saw Jenny's stricken face, then said more softly, 'Dad's right. What's done is done.'

'So you both think it was my candle?' Jenny said hoarsely.

'There seems to be no other reasonable explanation, lass,' her father said gently.

Jenny looked at him. He was looking at her so sadly that it made her want to cry. He wasn't blaming her. He wasn't angry with her. He simply didn't believe her – and who could blame him? As he had said, what other explanation was there? Marion Stewart obviously thought it was Jenny's fault too . . .

Jenny didn't know what to think any more. Maybe everyone else was right! Maybe she *had* caused the fire that had destroyed Windy Hill. She couldn't bear it!

Jenny looked at the sky. There were heavy dark clouds and there was a cold edge to the wind, but they weren't snow clouds – yet. She shivered. It wouldn't be long until the snow clouds *did* appear – and then the snow. Time was running out for them all.

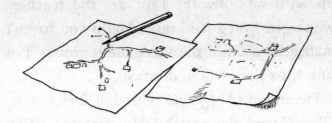

8

Fiona returned to school the following Monday. She looked so white and strained that, despite herself, Jenny felt a rush of sympathy for her. Fiona must have been very ill.

'Fiona,' she said, stopping the other girl in the corridor. 'Are you all right now?'

'What do *you* care?' Fiona replied, turning away.

Jenny reached out a hand and touched Fiona's

arm. 'It's just that you look so ill and worried,' she persisted. 'Are you concerned about catching up with schoolwork? I'm sure the teachers won't give you a hard time. And if you haven't managed to finish the Geography project, I'm sure Miss Kerr will understand.'

Fiona looked at Jenny with dull, lifeless eyes. 'The Geography project?' she repeated. 'Why are you talking about that?'

'They're due in today,' Jenny reminded her. 'I lost mine in the fire – and so did Ian, so we joined up with Carrie to do a joint one.'

Fiona took a step back, her eyes fixed on Jenny. Jenny noticed that her lips were dry and cracked and her hand trembled as she pushed a strand of hair behind her ear. But suddenly, she came to life.

'Mind your own business,' she snapped as she pushed past.

Later, in Geography, Jenny was miles away, thinking about Windy Hill.

'Hey! Wake up,' Carrie said, giving her a dig in the ribs. 'You're getting as bad as Fiona.'

'What do you mean?' said Jenny.

'Haven't you noticed?' Carrie said. 'She's acting really strangely today. She jumps every time anyone speaks to her.'

Jenny frowned. 'Well, I tried talking to her this morning and it was like talking to a zombie. Then I mentioned our Geography project and she just bit my head off and walked away.'

'Maybe it's because she knows our project is going to be the best in the class,' Carrie announced confidently.

'There's nothing like modesty!' Ian joked from the desk behind.

Jenny laughed. Carrie was always so positive. 'I hope Miss Kerr likes it.'

Part of the project had been to make a map of the Greybridge area, and then mark in the routes they all took to school, to friends' houses, to the shops and to other villages. Now Miss Kerr got the class to help her push several tables together so that they could lay out all the maps.

'That's amazing,' Ian said, pointing to the criss-crossing routes marked on the maps. 'We've managed to cover the whole area. Look at all the tracks we've got.'

The collection of maps was certainly

impressive. Between them the class had mapped out a complete circular area around the school.

'You should be able to see how many new routes you take and the new friends you've made since you came to Greybridge,' Miss Kerr said.

'Look!' Amy Jarrow said. 'There aren't any paths to this house.' Amy bent over the map. 'Dunraven,' she said. 'Who lives there?'

Fiona coughed and everyone looked at her. 'Me,' she said in a strained voice.

'You were supposed to put in the routes you take to your friends' houses,' Amy said helpfully. Then she frowned. 'Hey, nobody's put in any routes on their maps to your house, either . . .'

'That can't be right,' Miss Kerr said, smiling. 'Look again, Amy.'

Fiona made a strangled sound and rushed from the room. Amy looked aghast.

Miss Kerr looked around the class. 'Would someone go after her and see that she's all right? Are any of you friends with Fiona?'

There were long moments of silence as everyone looked at one another. Nobody offered.

'I thought she had just forgotten to put in her routes,' Amy said quietly. 'But it's true, isn't it?

Fiona *doesn't* have any friends.'

'Jenny?' Miss Kerr said. 'How about you? You volunteered to ask after Fiona when she was ill.'

Jenny knew she had to say yes. She nodded stiffly, then stood up. Carrie threw her a look of sympathy.

'Thank you, Jenny,' Miss Kerr said. 'Just see that she's OK. She doesn't need to come back to class until she feels better.'

Jenny closed the classroom door behind her and went in search of Fiona. It was the last thing she wanted to do at the moment.

She tried the girls' toilets first but there was no sign of her there. Then she thought of the cloakroom. Sure enough, Jenny found Fiona there, huddled in a corner.

'Fiona,' she said. 'Are you all right? Do you want to talk?'

Fiona turned to her, her face streaked with tears. 'What are *you* doing here?' she said, her voice catching.

'Miss Kerr asked me to come and see that you were all right,' Jenny replied.

Fiona's face twisted. 'I don't have any friends, do I? Everybody can see that now.'

Jenny didn't say anything for a while. 'People are worried about you,' she said at last. She hesitated. 'Especially Paul,' she continued. 'He says you've been having nightmares . . .'

Fiona whirled round. 'You've no right to go talking about me behind my back!' she said. 'Just leave me alone, do you hear me? Leave me alone!' And, with that, she rushed from the cloakroom.

Jenny stood for a moment, uncertain what to do. Well, Fiona certainly didn't want to discuss her problems. She sighed and trudged back to the classroom to report to Miss Kerr.

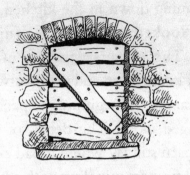

9

Fiona didn't appear at school the next day and, at the end of the week, Miss Kerr announced that Fiona would be off school until further notice.

Jenny and Ian went up to Windy Hill on Saturday morning to help Fraser and Matt move some ewes out of the fields and into the stables for shelter. The weather had turned so wet that the lower field was getting waterlogged.

Ellen Grace had accompanied them to do some more cleaning down in the kitchen.

Jenny looked around the ruined farm buildings. The upstairs windows of the house were now boarded up and the paintwork on the sills and frames was beginning to peel away from the damaged wood. The debris of the ruined lambing barn still lay where it had collapsed, its blackened timbers mingling with a heap of roof tiles that had been removed from the house roof for safety. It looked so desolate, it made Jenny want to cry. She hated to see Windy Hill in this state.

She was also finding it difficult to talk to Matt. He still seemed to blame her for the fire. They had always been the best of friends but now there seemed to be a shadow between them.

'When are the repairs going to start, Dad?' she asked, as her father called Jake and Nell to heel. Jess came bounding over with them.

'Well, Bob Elliott now wants an independent report,' Fraser Miles said in disgust.

'But what for?' Jenny asked. 'The weather is getting worse all the time and December is less than a week away. We'll have to leave Cliff House then! Where are we going to live while the repairs are being done?'

'I've been asking around,' her father said. 'There's a cottage on the other side of Graston that we could take, but the rent is high and it's too far away from Windy Hill for my liking. Still, we might have to go for that. Christmas is a bad time of year to be looking for a place to stay – especially since we only want a short-term let.'

'And it'll mean spending more money,' Matt put in. 'If things go on like this there's no way we'll get the insurance sorted out before Christmas. This is just what we need!'

Jenny flushed as her brother couldn't stop himself from giving her an accusing look. 'Matt . . .' she began pleadingly, but he turned away from her as a car drew into the farmyard. Jess sprang up and ran to meet it.

'That's Mrs McLay,' Ian said, surprised. 'Fiona is with her.'

'Fiona?' said Jenny. 'What on earth is *she* doing here?'

Jess ran up to Mrs McLay as she opened the car door, then backed away and growled as Fiona got out of the passenger seat. Hanging on to her mother's arm, Fiona followed Anna McLay over. She looked terribly pale and drawn, even worse then she had at school.

'Here, Jess,' Jenny called.

Jess came to her side slowly and sat in front of her, placing himself between her and Fiona, his eyes never leaving Fiona's face.

'I think Jess feels the same way about Fiona as we do,' Ian whispered as Jess gave another soft growl.

As the two visitors came close, Anna McLay bent and stroked Jess's muzzle. Jess wagged his tail and licked Mrs McLay's hand, but kept a wary eye on Fiona.

Then Mrs McLay looked up at the others. Her eyes resting on Fraser, she flushed bright red and shook her head. 'Oh, Fraser . . .' she started, haltingly. 'I found something out last night . . . something you need to know . . . But I honestly don't know where to start,' she said. 'I feel so mortified . . .' She drew Fiona forward and swallowed hard. 'Fiona has something to tell you.'

Jenny looked at Fiona in puzzlement. The girl

was looking at the house — at the smoke-blackened walls, the tiles missing from the roof, the boarded-up windows. Then she looked towards the pile of debris where the lambing barn had once stood and her face grew even paler.

'I didn't know it was as bad as this,' she said in a low voice. 'I haven't been here since the night of the bonfire.'

Jenny frowned. 'But you weren't here on Bonfire Night,' she said. 'You didn't come to the party.'

Fiona swallowed hard and clasped her hands together. 'Yes, I did,' she said. 'I came down to see what was happening.'

'We didn't see you,' Ian said, looking puzzled.

Fiona shook her head. She was clearly finding it difficult to speak. 'I didn't come up to the bonfire,' she went on at last. 'I just came to the house.'

'What?' said Jenny.

Fiona's head drooped. Her voice was so low they could hardly hear her. 'I wanted to watch,' she said. Silent tears began to course down her face. She wiped them away then took a long

shuddering breath. 'I started the fire at Windy Hill,' she said brokenly.

Jenny gasped. *Fiona*! She couldn't believe what she had just heard.

'I think you'd better tell us everything, Fiona,' Fraser Miles said quietly.

Fiona began to sob. 'I felt really jealous of everybody else having fun at the bonfire,' she said, in a strangled voice. 'I thought about how much everyone would be enjoying themselves.'

'But I asked you to come,' Jenny protested.

Fiona shook her head. 'Only because you felt sorry for me,' she said.

'That isn't true, Fiona,' Jenny insisted.

Fiona shook her head again, as if she didn't believe Jenny. 'I sneaked over to Windy Hill to watch,' she went on. 'But that made me feel even more lonely and left out of things. I had some sparklers and matches with me and I lit some of the sparklers, then I crept into the house to have a look around. I went upstairs to Jenny's bedroom. I took the sparklers and the matches with me.'

Jenny remembered the sparklers the fire

officer had found in her bedroom. So they had been Fiona's.

'And you just set fire to the bedroom?' Matt asked, his face red with anger.

Fiona shook her head. 'No! It wasn't like that at all! I didn't mean to,' she said. 'I opened the window to see the fireworks better. I lit another sparkler. Then I saw your Geography project work on your desk, Jenny. It made me angry and jealous. There wasn't a single track to Dunraven on your map but there were lots of tracks between Windy Hill and loads of other houses and farms around. The sparkler went out but I didn't want to put on the light in case anyone saw me so I lit a candle to see the map better. The candle flame caught on the papers . . .' Fiona looked at her mother.

Anna McLay nodded support and Fiona continued.

'I . . . just watched it . . . all your project stuff burning up. But the fire seemed to spread so fast and I got frightened. Then I started to choke on the smoke. I panicked. Jess was barking. He must have heard me. I ran out of the door and down the stairs and right out of the house. Jess was barking all the time. He knew what I had done.'

'So that's why Jess has been acting strangely around you,' Jenny said. 'He knew you had started the fire.'

Fiona looked at Jenny, her eyes huge and dark in her gaunt, tormented face. 'I'm so, so sorry,' she said, her voice breaking again.

'I think we know the rest,' Anna McLay said, wearily. 'The fire took hold and by the time Jess alerted Jenny it was too late to save the house.'

'Or the lambing barn,' Fraser Miles said softly.

Fiona was sobbing again now, but Jenny barely noticed. She felt a great rush of anger. 'You let everybody think it was my fault!' she cried. 'You even accused me yourself. How could you do that, Fiona? What have I ever done to make you hate me so much?'

Fiona couldn't answer. She simply turned away, burying her face in her mother's shoulder.

Fraser Miles laid a hand on Jenny's arm and Jenny looked at him. The anger left her as soon as it had arrived. One thought filled her mind. *It hadn't been her fault. She hadn't been responsible for the fire.* All the guilt she had been feeling was gone. Yes, Windy Hill still lay in ruins about them

. . . but *she* hadn't destroyed it – and Jess had known that. He had tried to tell her who had been the guilty one.

But now, as Anna McLay led the still-sobbing Fiona to the car and settled her in the passenger seat, Jess remained silent. He seemed to understand that Fiona no longer posed a threat. Anna McLay walked back across the farmyard towards them. 'Fiona needed to confess,' she said, quietly. 'But I think she's had enough for one day.'

Mrs McLay drew herself up and looked directly at Fraser, her eyes pleading. 'Calum and I will, of course, take full financial responsibility for all the damage,' she went on, 'including the lambing barn. I know it wasn't insured, Fraser, but it will be rebuilt at our expense. If you want to prosecute . . .' Here, Anna McLay's voice broke. 'I know how it looks, Fraser,' she said falteringly. 'But you must believe me. It wasn't arson. Fiona didn't set fire to the house deliberately. You've seen how ill she's made herself worrying about what she did. I think she is truly sorry.' Anna McLay's voice broke off altogether.

Fraser returned her gaze. 'There's one thing I want to make clear,' he said. 'I don't want any more delays on the insurance settlement. I can't prove anything but I'm pretty sure Calum has been holding things up in the hope that I'll sell out to him. You can tell him from me, Anna, that it won't work. If I don't get that insurance claim tied up and settled tomorrow then I'm going to make things very sticky for him.'

Anna McLay flushed a deep red. 'I didn't know he'd been holding things up, Fraser,' she said. 'But he has been seeing a lot of Bob Elliot recently . . .' She frowned. 'Don't worry. He'll stop interfering now – and he'll build you the best lambing barn in the Borders. I'll see to that.'

'And what about Fiona?' Jenny asked quietly. 'What's going to happen to her?'

Anna McLay shook her head, the tears finally spilling over. 'I don't know, Jenny,' she said. 'That depends on you and your family. I hope that when you've had time to consider, you will agree that she's punished herself enough, without taking matters further. She was very wrong to put the blame on you – and she knows that. It took so much for her to come here today. I hope some day you'll be able to forgive her.'

Jenny didn't say anything. At that moment, she could never imagine forgiving Fiona.

'That's a lot to ask,' Fraser Miles said, putting his arm round Jenny's shoulder.

'I know it is,' Mrs McLay said. 'It's just that Fiona is a very sick girl and I'm worried about her.'

Fraser Miles nodded. 'Of course you are, Anna,' he said. After a pause, he said, 'I won't prosecute. Fiona is only a child and an unhappy one at that. But I won't stand any more nonsense from Calum.'

Anna McLay looked at him. 'Calum will behave himself,' she said firmly. 'Fiona nearly ruined you, Fraser. She made all of you homeless and caused Jenny terrible distress . . . But I'm going to do everything in my power to make it up to you all. I promise you that.'

Matt ran a hand through his hair. 'One problem that isn't solved is where we're going to live while the repairs are carried out. The Turners have guests coming for Christmas and New Year so we can't stay on at Cliff House.

And Dad needs to be near the farm to look after the sheep.'

'But you *can* be near Windy Hill, Fraser,' Anna McLay said. 'That was the other thing I came to tell you. We can offer you a home while Windy Hill is repaired.'

'At Dunraven?' Jenny said, unable to hide her horror.

Anna McLay coloured. 'Not exactly,' she said. 'No, I was talking about Thistle Cottage, the one Mrs Grace used to rent.'

Anna looked at Ellen Grace, who'd come out to see what was happening, and flushed again. Everyone knew that Calum McLay had refused to renew the lease on Thistle Cottage for Mrs Grace out of pure spite – because she'd gone to work for the Mileses. It had lain empty ever since, but things had worked out for the best despite Calum, because Ellen Grace had found a better home at Windy Hill.

Ellen Grace nodded encouragingly, and Mrs McLay went on. 'As you know, the cottage is quite near the boundary between Dunraven and Windy Hill and all it needs is a good airing and it'll be fit for you to live in.' She looked at Fraser.

'I know it isn't ideal, Fraser, but it was all I could think of. Calum will ensure that repairs to Windy Hill are done in double-quick time, and then you'll all be able to move back home.'

'That's very kind of you, Anna,' Mrs Grace said gently. 'But there really won't be enough room for us all at Thistle Cottage. There are four of us – five if you count Matt. He comes home at weekends.'

'You don't have to count me,' Ian reminded her. 'I'm going to Canada for Christmas and New Year to see Mum and Dad.'

Mrs Grace nodded. 'That's true,' she said. 'That'll help.'

'Well, perhaps, Ellen, you wouldn't mind a bed at Dunraven . . .?' Anna McLay suggested hesitantly. 'It's only a few minutes' walk from the cottage.'

Mrs Grace smiled and nodded. 'Thank you, Anna. That would be fine by me.' She looked at Fraser Miles. He nodded acceptance too.

Breathing a sigh of relief, Anna McLay continued. 'Well, that's sorted, then.' She looked round. 'I'd better get Fiona home now. And then Calum and I will get started on putting things right.' She walked over to her car, saying, 'Goodbye – and thank you. I'll be in touch shortly.'

'Taking Thistle Cottage means we'll all be separated,' Jenny said quietly, as Anna McLay drove off.

Fraser Miles put a hand on Jenny's shoulder. 'It looks like we'll just have to put up with it, lass. It's a roof over our heads. I'll get on to Marion Stewart first thing Monday morning and get things moving.'

Jenny nodded and put a hand on Jess's head. She wished that Mrs Grace didn't have to sleep at Dunraven, especially as Ian was going to be away in Canada. Still, she had Jess. At least she wouldn't be separated from him.

She looked at her father. He seemed to be waiting for her approval. Jess pushed his nose into Jenny's hand and she bent down to him, stroking his ears. 'What do you think, Jess?' she asked. Jess licked her hand, as if in encouragement. Jenny laughed. Her head came up. 'Let's do it,' she said. 'The sooner we get started, the sooner we can move back home.' For the first time, she felt confident that Windy

Hill would rise from the ashes.

'Too right,' said Matt. 'And not only will the insurance pay for the house and stables to be made as good as new, Calum McLay will build us a new lambing barn.'

'And, best of all,' Jenny added quietly, 'you know now that the fire wasn't my fault.'

Matt turned to Jenny. 'Jen,' he said. 'I'm so sorry I doubted you.'

Ian nodded sheepishly.

'We're all sorry,' Fraser Miles said.

'Do you forgive us?' Matt asked.

Jenny gave him a hug. 'Of course I do,' she assured him.

Ellen Grace put an arm round Jenny's shoulders. 'Well, thank goodness for that,' she said. 'You've got quite a girl here, Fraser,' she said, looking at Mr Miles.

'I know that, Ellen,' he replied gruffly.

Jenny grinned and laid her hand on Jess's head. 'And Jess is quite a dog! He was trying to tell us all the time who had started the fire.'

'Trust Jess,' said her father. 'Sometimes I think he's the best thing that's happened to Windy Hill.'

'Oh, he is,' Jenny declared. 'Aren't you, boy? The very best!'

Jenny looked around the farm – her home – and raised her face to the wind. Her voice floated over the ruined buildings and on up into the air. 'We'll be back soon,' she said. 'I promise – we'll be back!'

ORDER FORM

Lucy Daniels

0 340 70438 1	JESS THE BORDER COLLIE 1: *THE ARRIVAL*	£3.99 ❏
0 340 70439 X	JESS THE BORDER COLLIE 2: *THE CHALLENGE*	£3.99 ❏
0 340 70440 3	JESS THE BORDER COLLIE 3: *THE RUNAWAY*	£3.99 ❏
0 340 73595 3	JESS THE BORDER COLLIE 4: *THE BETRAYAL*	£3.99 ❏
0 340 73596 1	JESS THE BORDER COLLIE 5: *THE SACRIFICE*	£3.99 ❏
0 340 73597 X	JESS THE BORDER COLLIE 6: *THE HOMECOMING*	£3.99 ❏

All Hodder Children's books are available at your local bookshop, or can be ordered direct from the publisher. Just tick the titles you would like and complete the details below. Prices and availability are subject to change without prior notice.

Please enclose a cheque or postal order made payable to *Bookpoint Ltd*, and send to: Hodder Children's Books, 39 Milton Park, Abingdon, OXON OX14 4TD, UK.
Email Address: orders@bookpoint.co.uk

If you would prefer to pay by credit card, our call centre team would be delighted to take your order by telephone. Our direct line *01235 400414* (lines open 9.00 am–6.00 pm Monday to Saturday, 24 hour message answering service). Alternatively you can send a fax on *01235 400454*.

TITLE		FIRST NAME		SURNAME	

ADDRESS	

DAYTIME TEL:		POST CODE	

If you would prefer to pay by credit card, please complete:
Please debit my Visa/Access/Diner's Card/American Express (delete as applicable) card no:

Signature ....Expiry Date: ....

If you would NOT like to receive further information on our products please tick the box. ❏